THE
SILO

THE SILO

A NOVEL

G.S. HEIST

Copyright © 2024 by G.S. Heist

The Silo

All rights reserved. No part of this publication may be scanned, uploaded, reproduced, distributed, or transmitted in any form or by any means, including photocopying, recording, or other electronic or mechanical methods, without the prior written permission from the author, except as permitted by U. S. copyright law.

Printed in United States of America

This is a work of fiction. The views expressed herein are the sole responsibility of the author. The story, all names, characters, and incidents portrayed in this production are a product of the author's imagination, and any resemblance to actual persons, living or dead, or actual events or locations, is entirely coincidental.

ISBN: 979-8-9907963-0-0

Cover and interior design by Christian Storm

Edited by Ellen Coughtrey

First edition (2024)

For Jack, Ethan, Margot and Caden

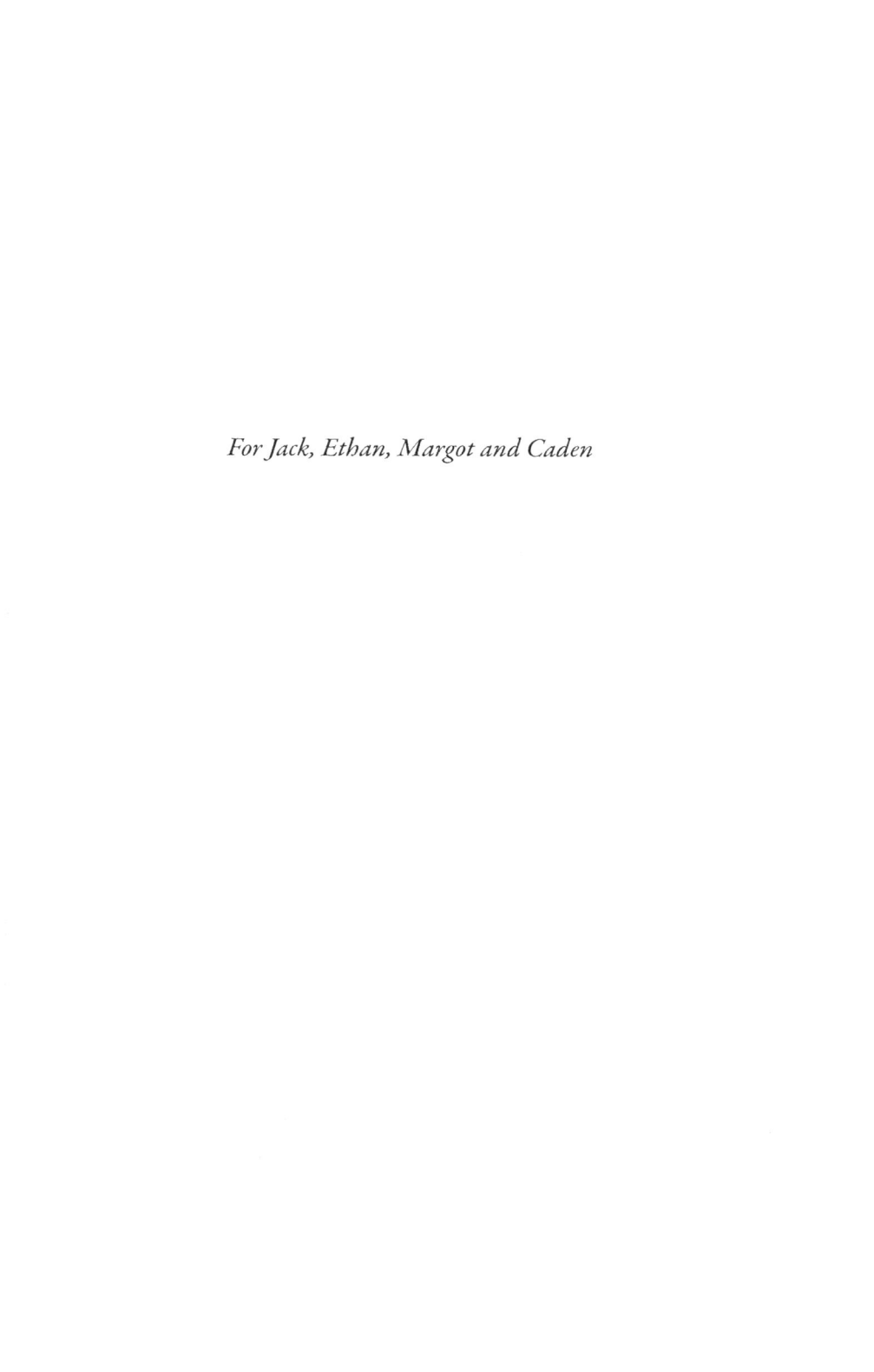

CONTENTS

PROLOGUE 5

ONE 7
TWO 16
THREE 25
FOUR 34
FIVE 45
SIX 51
SEVEN 62
EIGHT 71
NINE 83
TEN 97
ELEVEN 103
TWELVE 120
THIRTEEN 128
FOURTEEN 136
FIFTEEN 145
SIXTEEN 150

ACKNOWLEDGEMENTS 159
ABOUT THE AUTHOR 160

THE SILO

"He stared into that relentless circle of fire, a witness to its blood melting into the horizon. He hoped her death shadow would fade into oblivion, but it remained a stubborn stain forever stamped onto his soul's memory."

— **G.S. HEIST**

PROLOGUE

THE SUMMER SUN struggled to break through the evening haze that hovered over the expansive fields, dotting the rural farm county. The fading sun's golden hue mimicked the shade of flowing wheat-beards. Creating a soft blanket of waves rising and falling like a bright white cotton sheet, billowing in the soft August breeze as it hangs from a secluded clothesline. The sun was burning relentless, endless, and perpetual, its color gradually changing from gold to violent red, a deep pigeon-blood red, flowing like lava outward from nature's perfect circle. A raging ball of fire sinking and submitting to evening rest; softening, giving off a pleasant glow revealing a singular ominous figure. There was a lonely silhouette, disappearing and reappearing to the naked eye, as the daylight gave way to darkness; yielding secrets, surrendering the mysteries, and illuminating the truth exposed by a single aging silo.

One old man, a graying cattle farmer in his eighties, taking his usual evening drive into town in his 1962 Chevy pickup truck, down Old Johnson Road, noticed something, or someone, high upon the silo. Something unusual caught his eye, perhaps nothing but his old mind playing tricks; not anything to cause him to take his eyes off the dusty gravel road for more than a second or two. He knew the Weaver's farm, which the silo belonged. He had heard the stories. He paid little attention. He was too old for the rumor mill, but the rumors persisted. The old man could not know what he saw. His mind protected his soul's fragility. Whatever he saw, it changed nothing. Life would go on.

ONE

TEN HOURS EARLIER Detective Frank Braun was cleaning out the bottom drawer of his desk and came across several handwritten notes from his final lecture on interviewing and interrogating homicide suspects. The same questions crossed his mind. Throw them away? Save them? Frank read to himself the final paragraph:

Interviewing and interrogation are more than just words spoken between two people. There are complex body movements involved. The eyes, facial muscles, arms, hands and legs, and feet must be instantly studied. What is the overall demeanor of the person? Does the body language link to the words that are spoken? Communication is a two-way street. How is the person responding to your questions? If you get a chance to interview or interrogate a suspect in a crime, allow them to expose themselves. Their words, their body language, their overall demeanor will speak volumes as to who they are and what they are and why they are. Between the spoken word and the unspoken communication, and of course your relentless persistence, a confession may just unfold in front of your eyes.

BRAUN ALWAYS BELIEVED in a philosophy of allowing the truth to develop over time and passed along this knowledge at conferences and training seminars on the art of homicide investigation. He kept an open mind and held no preconceived opinions of those he interviewed, even if they were accused of something deadly serious. He once told a rookie detective, never tell suspects who or what they are. Never force out of them what you would like to hear. Let them reveal, in their own time, the answers to those questions and perhaps the crimes they have committed. Frank Braun was about to retire. He would leave his career with a combination of nostalgia, pride and even some regret. He was not openly happy about retirement. Some believed he really did not want to go. Giving up the chase was difficult.

Detective Braun's desk phone rang five times. He resisted answering it. After all, this was his last day at work. Why get caught up in something new? Out of habit he gave in.

"Detective Braun."

"Frank. I know you don't want to be bothered," the desk sergeant began, "but, we got a guy in jail. Needs to be interviewed."

"Have him talk to Jenkins," Braun bluntly replied. "It's my last day. I'm cleaning out my desk. I don't want to get caught up in something I can't finish."

"Captain says you need to talk to this guy."

"Need to?" Braun asked, now tapping his pen on his desk. "Why me?"

"He just said everyone else was out on cases," the sergeant huffed. "This guy did ask for you by name, Doc. Acts like he knows you. He's very anxious about something. He has been pacing the cell floor since he got here."

Braun's silence communicated his lack of enthusiasm. He could hear the desk sergeant talking to someone else in the background, obviously dealing with two situations at the same time. "He says he knows me?"

"He asked for you, Frank. Said it was important," the sergeant repeated. "He's very jittery. That's the best way to describe him. He's an anxious man. Sorry to dump this on you on your last day. He won't talk to anyone else."

"Place him in interview room one," Braun sighed, loud enough for the sergeant to get the message. "I'll be there in a few minutes. But I don't plan on getting involved in a new case."

Interview room one was only eight by ten feet at the most. The large concrete block walls were brush painted, if you consider dark gray a color of paint. The floor was made of basic, speckled twelve-inch asbestos tiles, worn and dirty from years of shoe bottoms and aggressive pacing. Lighting was dim, but adequate. Bright enough for the discreet camera placed high in the far corner of the room. The camera faced the interviewee. The ceiling was roughly nine feet high, with acoustic tiles measuring thirty-six by eighteen inches. They were stained a deep yellow, almost to the point of mustard brown, from a time long ago when smoking was allowed in this room. Braun missed the days when smoking was legal. He recalled how suspects, back when he started, were far less likely to clam up if they had a distraction, like a nerve-soothing cigarette between their fingers. Sometimes, during tough interrogations, he had no problem looking the other way. A smoke-filled room was well worth clinching a solid confession.

There was a small simple table in the middle of the room. The table was wooden, probably pine, and seemed shorter than most. There were two simple walnut-stained chairs. The seats of the chairs had no padding. Comfort was antithetical to their purpose. People entered this room to be questioned, probed, and prodded, and challenged in their way of thinking. Their wills would be tested to tell a story their way, even if it was not the truth. Persuasion was the hallmark of interviewing and interrogation. Part of the persuasion involved the carrots. The carrot was often more important than the stick. Detectives knew this and suspects should have known this. Once words were drawn from their mouths, keeping those words flowing becomes paramount. Braun knew that sticks could not only ruin the pace, but could completely stop the flow of any conversation.

A young man sat upright at the table on one of the chairs. Both elbows rested on the table and his hands were firmly clenched, fingers intertwined. He was anxious. That was not uncommon. It meant very little at this point. Detective Braun entered the room. The young man looked up. Before speaking, Braun set a tape recorder on the table, along with a pad of yellow-lined paper and two ink pens. Nothing more. The young man seemed to stare. Braun's hair was a mixture of gray and brown. He was dressed casually. Beige slacks, white button-down collared dress shirt and a blue sport coat and brown leather dress shoes, many miles worn down the soles. He tried hard not to come off as intimidating. As far as Braun knew, they had never met.

"I'm Detective Frank Braun. You can call me Frank. Detective Braun if you like."

"Thank you."

"What would you like me to call you?"

"I'm Jacob Weaver. Jacob is fine."

"Jacob it is," Braun said. "Can I get you anything, Jacob? Coffee, water, or soda?"

"I overheard that officer out there call you Doc," Jacob said.

"Don't worry about that." Braun cleared his throat.

"I'm curious now," he said. "Why did he call you Doc?"

"He calls me Doc. Just a nickname he has for me."

"Where'd that come from?"

"It's just a nickname."

"There can be a lot behind a nickname," Jacob pressed. "Why Doc?"

"If you have to know," Braun said, "he always said that whenever I interview someone, I sound more like a psychologist than a detective. That's it. Just a personal thing. Just his silly nickname for me. Nothing more. Now, do you want something to drink?"

Detective Braun wanted to make Jacob comfortable, but he also couldn't help but exude a certain amount of impatience. Braun's mind was focused on packing-up and getting on with his pending retirement. He really didn't want to get stuck with a lengthy interview.

"Water," he said. Jacob watched Braun with curiosity, like he was studying him.

"Don't care for coffee?"

"I drink coffee, but I use too much sugar."

"I have sugar if you want it," Braun offered as he glanced down, studying a computer print-out. He was trying to read what was in front of him and still pay attention to Jacob.

"Water is fine."

"No problem." Braun finished reading the print-out, which was Jacob Weaver's most recent criminal history. He didn't have time to examine it closely, but it gave him some sense of who was sitting across the table.

"Do you have a bathroom I could use, Detective?" Jacob squirmed.

"It's right around the corner," Braun pointed. "Go ahead and use it. I'll be right back with your water."

"I changed my mind," Jacob said. "I will have that coffee. Two sugars if you have it. No problem if you don't. I can drink it black."

"Coffee, two sugars," Braun sighed. He worried about this guy's wishy-washy demeanor. He couldn't seem to make up his mind.

Detective Braun tilted his head, barely shook it, and grinned. He came back with a coffee, two sugars and a glass of water.

Jacob returned shortly. Braun thought he looked pale. Perhaps, nerves were getting the best of him. He seemed worried. Braun had his own theories. Jacob wasn't the first man he had ever interviewed. With a drunken driving charge hanging over his head, and another count for possessing cannabis, Jacob was starting to sweat his predicament. The two drinks were placed on the table in front of Jacob's chair. Braun hoped the guy wouldn't faint.

"Thanks."

"You're welcome," Braun said. "So, let's talk about why you're here, Jacob."

"You probably want to know why I'm drunk so early in the day," Jacob guessed. "I really didn't have that much to drink."

"That's a good place to start," Braun said. "How old are you?"

"I am almost thirty. I have a birthday coming up, soon."

Braun refrained from smiling, though he thought about how a child wants you to know they are nine and a half and not just nine. It made him think of his own kids, even though they were grown.

"Don't take this the wrong way, but you don't look that old."

"I get that all the time," Jacob said. "I have always looked younger than I am. A curse, I guess."

"You won't see it that way when you're older," Braun smiled. "You'll be happy someday that you have youthful genes."

Jacob came across as a lost soul to Braun. Not so young, but immature. Yet, his criminal record seemed to tell a different story. Braun wondered about this stark contrast. He gave Jacob his Miranda warnings. Jacob listened intently and told Braun he understood them, telling him he still wanted to talk. He refused an attorney.

"Jacob, I am more interested in the cannabis that was found in your vehicle." Braun looked straight into Jacob's eyes for his reaction.

"Cannabis? Not sure what you're talking about. The weed you mean?" Jacob quickly straightened up in his chair. "That's just for me. It's mine. You know, personal use. I will admit that I smoke weed once in a while. It keeps me calm. I won't lie about that."

"I know what personal use is," Braun said, "but, there are several separate packages in that shoebox they removed from your trunk. Prosecutors know exactly what that means. Looks like you're selling this to people. You are looking at a possible felony here. The DUI is not your only worry."

"I give it to some people I know. Just a few," he explained. "I'm not a dealer if that's what you're insinuating."

"You could be looking at some serious time behind bars."

"Time? Prison time?" Jacob noticeably slumped. He leaned forward and placed his face in his hands. "For this? I drank a little. No one was hurt. The marijuana is mine."

"I can't say what the prosecutor will do," Braun explained, "but there is a law that you should be very concerned about."

"A law? What do you mean? What law?"

"It concerns your criminal history. You have a couple of felonies on your record." Braun seemed to be revealing something Jacob had never seriously considered before. He couldn't deny it, but it was as if he never truly understood what had happened to him back in his late teens and early twenties. And why it could come back and haunt him someday. "There is something called the three strikes law."

"Three strikes?"

"You might be looking at a very long time in prison." Braun glanced again at the criminal history and scrunched his eyes and shook his head. "Some people have been convicted of the three strikes law and are spending the rest of their lives behind bars."

Jacob stared. It seemed like Braun was talking to a child that had nowhere to run. Jacob couldn't quite grasp the severity of his past crimes. They were coming back to haunt him now.

"What can I do?" he asked. "What can I say?"

"All prosecutors ever want is good solid information."

"Information? What kind of information?" Braun noticed a tear stream down Jacob's cheek. Jacob wiped it away with the back of his hand. It was as if he didn't want Braun to think less of him. "I told you I was drunk. I told you the weed was mine. I'm confessing. I am telling the truth. That's not good enough?"

"You may be looking at a life sentence," Braun lectured, leaning forward, toward Jacob. "They will want something from you. They'll want something serious. Something extremely important. Unless you have a big player in the drug world that provides you with your dope, you might be hung out to dry on this three strikes law."

Jacob sat way back in his chair, creating physical distance, allowing the emotional space he needed to catch his breath. The thought of spending his life in prison suddenly slapped him across the face. He crossed his arms, locking them firmly and closing off his upper body from Braun's harsh reality check.

"I see now. I am completely fucked. That's what you're saying. There's no escaping the reality of my situation." Jacob stood and turned his back on Braun, as if rejecting his words would somehow negate their ugly truth. He ran both hands through his hair and let out a moan. "Jesus Christ! This can't be happening. This is all a bad dream. What in the hell is going on? A little beer and dope?"

"At this point, Jacob," Braun admitted, "an act of mercy by the prosecutor will be your only chance. Unless you can give her someone's head on a silver platter."

Detective Braun hoped this would be the end of his own involvement in this case, but he did feel sympathy for Jacob's plight. Braun had real problems with the three strikes law, but knew he had to always work within the justice system. The power and control of a case was not only taken away from an investigator, it was even taken away from judges. Laws such as these removed necessary discretion. Yet, Braun did as he was told. He interviewed the guy. He was up against the clock. Jacob's future was in the hands of the prosecutor's office and Braun had to get back to his desk and clear out. His retirement was imminent.

"I know what I have to do Detective Braun," Jacob said. "I just need a little time to gather my thoughts."

"I'm going to put you back in your cell," Braun explained. "I need to go to my desk. There are some things I must take care of. And I need to make some calls."

"Then what?" Jacob sighed, as if he knew the answer.

"I'm not quite sure, Jacob," Braun replied. "I really don't know."

Jacob went silent. He sat and stared. He glared up at Detective Braun. His brain was racing. Braun could tell. He waited for him to speak, but Jacob simply gazed for a couple more minutes. Jacob totally shut down. Braun led him by the arm, back into his cell. The crash of steel colliding with steel as the door slammed caused Jacob to flinch. For him, it was the sound of torture.

TWO

JACOB PACED BACK AND FORTH in his cell, like a caged wolf. He looked around, imagining the rest of his life in a cold concrete pen. He knew he would never last. The walls were hard and damp to the touch. He noticed the mattress, which sat upon a large poured concrete base, was only four inches thick and lacked anything remotely close to comfort. The bars were solid steel, thick, intimidating and a constant reminder that Jacob would be staring out and not in. His mind went in so many directions he could not seem to focus on one single thought.

He sat on that yellowing, flattened thing called a mattress, hands in his face, and began to cry. Jacob came to the realization that his entire life had led up to this human disaster. *Why me?* He asked himself. He took four or five deep breaths. He felt his anxiety building. Another reminder that he could not live with panic attacks in prison. That would be a sign to the pack of wolves around him that he was weak. He would be a target for everything unseemly that was a reality in the penitentiary. Jacob calmed his heartbeat and his breathing and began to reflect. *What about the others in my life that sent me down this road? Why am I in this mess alone?* He knew that he had to tell his story. The story of Jacob.

Detective Braun returned from his office and approached the cell. He led Jacob back to the interview room so they could continue talking. As much as Braun wanted to move on toward his new life, there was something about Jacob that wouldn't let him walk away without some sense of closure. Jacob sat down and looked up at Braun. He had the feeling Jacob was looking at his only lifeline.

Jacob sat back and crossed his arms. "You really don't remember me, do you?"

This took Braun by surprise. There was something familiar about Jacob, but he could not pinpoint what was causing this curiosity.

"I'm not sure, Jacob," he squinted. "Have we met before?"

"I was only twelve," he began. "I decided to run away from the farm. My aunt called you people. You were driving down Old Johnson Road in one of your black and whites. A big cherry on top. You found me about two miles away from the farm. I thought I had made it far, but my escape route was not exactly unpredictable."

"Maybe you wanted someone to find you."

"That could be, but you weren't very helpful, Detective," Jacob jabbed. He seemed pissed off at Braun. Revealing his true feelings, at this point, caused Braun to listen closer. There was something intriguing about Jacob. His demeanor changed in front of Braun's eyes. He decided to pull himself back into this case, psychologically, emotionally, and with the same passion he felt years ago, when his investigative skills changed people's lives.

"I wasn't?" Braun laid his pen down and listened. "What did I do? Or didn't do, Jacob?"

"As you drove me back to the farm, I told you I was scared to go back," Jacob admitted. "I wanted you to listen, but you did what all adults did with me. Ignored me. Took the words of adults over mine. You put me right back in the middle of the shit. You didn't give a damn, either."

"I'm sorry," Braun responded. He pulled his chair from the opposite side of the table and placed it right next to Jacob. Braun understood that closer contact was a sign of empathy. "I'm listening to you now."

"There are things about my family," he quietly began. "Things families shouldn't do. Things children shouldn't see. At first, I thought all kids lived this way. You know, were disciplined like I was. Kids always assume other kids are raised the same way."

"Do you want to talk about your family now?" Braun asked. "Are you ready to talk about these things you are alluding to? I won't force you to relive anything, but it may help you now. With the predicament you're in. I just won't know. I can't know, until you reveal the things you're hiding."

Braun was intentionally tiptoeing around the words Jacob spoke. He anticipated what was beginning to unfold, but wanted Jacob to be the one that spoke the accusatory words. This was not a time for assumptions. He anticipated Jacob was referring to abuse of some kind, but he wanted to be careful and not lead Jacob down the wrong path. Braun did not know what Jacob was thinking. If he had been abused or forced to live in a dangerous environment, or even witnessed something he shouldn't have, Jacob had to tell Braun straight out. He was a grown man now. Not a child.

"I have stories about things. I have never been strong enough to tell anyone." Jacob shuddered for a moment.

Whatever haunted him lived just beneath his skin, ready to ooze out. Perhaps, this was the time to speak those words. Was Detective Braun the man to listen? Would these revelations free Jacob's soul? Even if he were not free to leave those four cold walls, which were beginning to haunt him?

"Where would you like to start, Jacob?"

"I need to tell you about my family," he said as he sat forward. "They are why I'm here."

Braun decided that there was no reason to push Jacob. He noticed that he had given up that powerful force of natural resistance. Having your own life on the line was quite the motivation to let the words flow. It may not be that easy, but for Jacob it was necessary. He knew it. Whatever he revealed to Braun would have to be verified and corroborated and then handed over to the prosecutor. Decisions, above Detective Braun's pay grade, would have to be made about the DUI, the possession of drugs and, most critically, the three strikes law. Jacob's life, his secret life, would eventually be on trial, even if it were quietly critiqued within the dim lit private office of a single lawyer. Those with the power and authority could cause a person's soul to hang in the balance. Jacob began to find himself in his own personal purgatory. A psychological limbo, created by a chain of events, had begun on the day he was born.

"Tell me how you ended up here." Braun reached out and pressed the record button on his tape recorder.

"I have lived with my grandmother and grandfather, on the Weaver family farm," he began, "off and on my entire life."

"Is Grandma still alive?"

"No."

"Grandfather?"

"He is dead. Seven years ago."

"I'm sorry to hear that."

Braun grabbed his pen and scratched down some notes. "Please ignore the writing, Jacob. I'll be taking some notes occasionally as we talk."

"That's part of life. Dying, I mean," Jacob answered. "He and I weren't very close anyway."

Jacob winced at the perceptible click, click, click from Braun's pen. "He raised you?"

"No. My aunt did," he answered. "And my grandmother, to a certain extent."

"What about your parents?"

Jacob sat frozen in place. Braun allowed him the time he needed. The pause was long. He noted the strange reaction to the word, parents.

"That sounds like a touchy subject," Braun deduced, lifting his eyes from the page.

"I didn't know my father," he whispered, as if ashamed. "So, I know nothing about him."

"And your mother?"

"I wish I didn't know anything about her."

"She wasn't much of a parent?"

"That's an understatement," he replied without hesitation. Jacob began sitting more erect in his chair, as if he took offense having to even consider her.

"It was that bad, huh?" Braun scratched on his pad, *mom a major problem*.

"As far as I'm concerned, she was useless."

"That bad?" Braun didn't want Jacob to ignore the impact of his mother on his life, even if it was negative. He needed a detailed history.

"Drugs, sex, men," he answered, looking down at the floor. "I had a, so-called, step-father. He was one of her many men. And there were many."

"They weren't married? You say there were many men."

"Not sure exactly," Jacob smirked at his own lack of knowledge. "They came and went."

"This guy was not exactly a good role model? As a father?" Braun pressed. He could tell that the subject of his mother and her exploits was something Jacob wanted to avoid. But Braun also knew this could be a major cause of the DUI and drug charge.

"They were perfect for each other," he exclaimed. "Both pieces of shit."

Braun scribbled *pieces of shit* on his notepad. "Any siblings?"

"No. Thank God," Jacob whispered. "I took enough abuse. I wouldn't want any brothers and sisters to go through what I went through."

"What kind of abuse?" Braun focused. "This is important, Jacob. Probably the toughest thing to talk about, but very important. Who abused you?"

"My grandfather was the one," he admitted, "but my grandmother stood by and did nothing. Acted like she didn't know. But, she did and sometimes I think that can be just as bad."

"What did he do?"

"It was a mental abuse," he described. "My grandfather was hard. He was tough. I can't say he had much of an emotional attachment to me. I was just someone taking up space on the farm. He worked me a lot, which I understood, to a point, because farmers work hard. But it was his discipline that caused me nightmares."

"Tell me what he did." Braun readied his pen.

"Grandpa had a thing about his silo. He used it to scare me," he explained.

Jacob shivered for a moment. Braun noticed. He could see that reliving this memory was still a powerful emotion that caused Jacob an outward physical reaction.

"When the silo was empty, he would make me take timeouts inside. If he thought I did something wrong or needed disciplining. He would padlock the door from the outside. I was never sure how long it would be before he let me out. Or if he was coming back at all. That's why I hate being in that cell."

"Describe it."

"It was dark. Sometimes hot and sometimes cold. It depended on the time of year. I would just pace inside. Waiting. Wondering when he'd be back. It's the not knowing that drives you crazy. I would look up to see if I could climb up and get out somehow. I was trapped like an animal. The longer I was in there the more nervous I got. Of course, I didn't know what anxiety was back then. On top of it, a kid has to go to the bathroom. Where do you go? I lost all control of me. Of my own mind."

"What happened when the silo was full?"

"That was even worse."

Jacob was beginning to sweat. This memory brought him to near panic. His breathing increased. "One time it was full of corn. Every farmer, and their families, knew that you needed to stay a long way from a silo full of grain, like corn, or wheat. If you fell in you could sink, like quicksand, and suffocate. I was only twelve at the time. According to Grandpa, I was playing on the silo. I was just climbing up the ladder, a little ways, then jumping off. He came over and grabbed me by the arm. He began to tie a long rope around my upper body, under my armpits. He would say, 'If you want to play on this silo, I'll let you.' He then made me climb up the steel ladder, as he followed me. He pushed me from behind and told me how much fun I would have. He opened a hatch at the top and told me to get in. The corn was almost over flowing. I knew that I could suffocate. He always hounded me about that. I knew he knew it, but he pushed me in anyway. I began to sink… slowly."

Braun listened intently. He was very familiar with this deadly killer. He was aware of many farmers and farmhands that had lost their lives in silos. It is like a massive pit of quicksand that pulls and pulls without compassion. Tons of loose grain has a way of grabbing your body, like the tentacles of a ruthless, unforgiving monster.

"My nightmares were coming true. The pressure on my legs was relentless. The corn pulled me down, hard, and violent. It felt like a python coiling its body around mine. Constricting me. In my twelve-year-old mind, there was no escape from the silo's grip. I was helpless. I got pulled downward clear to my hips and all I could think of was Grandpa letting go of the rope. If he did, I knew I was gone forever."

"What was your grandpa saying to you? Anything?"

"He was actually laughing," he replied. "He would say, 'Playing in the silo is fun isn't it, Jacob?'"

"Then what happened?"

"When the corn was clear up to my chest, he began to pull on the rope. The rope tightened around my chest and under my armpits. Squeezing my lungs. I couldn't breathe. I knew if the rope pulled up over my head, there would be nothing he could do to save me. His plan was to teach me a lesson. But I knew he realized it was more difficult to pull me out than he even thought. It was like he was in this bizarre form of tug-of-war with the silo. Battling an inanimate object. A monster. How do you fight something that has no feelings? No compassion? Grandpa struggled until he was finally able to pull me out, but he was sweating and breathing hard. I knew he almost lost me. In my nightmares, still to this day, I am convinced he doesn't have the strength to pull me out. He gives up the fight and lets go. I gradually sink, fighting for my next breath. And all I hear is his laughter."

"How do you deal with the nightmares?"

"I don't. I can't. How can you?" he asked. "I'll admit. That's why I smoke all that weed."

"Does it help?"

"It doesn't stop the panic attacks, if that's what you're asking."

THREE

DETECTIVE BRAUN LEFT the interview room and went back to his office. One line on his desk phone was flashing. He had been notified that an important call had come in and the person was placed on hold. It was the prosecutor. Braun was interested in her legal point of view. Jacob needed to know what he faced. She was new to the job. Braun did not know her very well. He was not sure how gung-ho she was to consider the three strikes law. If she wanted to make a name for herself as a hard-nosed attorney, this would be a slam-dunk case to pursue to reach that goal. So, it seemed. He hoped she was unbiased and analytical and would be able to see every angle in the case. For Braun, any legal opinion at this point would give him a sense of direction. Where was this going? Was Jacob's story leading somewhere significant? There was a lot more digging to do. The phone light blinked.

"This is Frank Braun."

"This is Catherine Thomas. The prosecutor in your case," she confirmed. "I'm calling about the guy with the DUI and dope."

"I'm interviewing him now."

"I will get straight to the point, Detective. If this goes to trial the DUI and drug charge will be handled by my assistant."

"What about the three strikes law aspect? Will you be the decision-maker regarding which direction that goes?"

"I will be, yes," she answered. Ms. Thomas got to the point. She seemed blunt. Braun liked that in a prosecutor.

"This kid is fragile," Braun explained. "He wouldn't last six months in a maximum-security prison."

"Kid? What kid? He is a grown man, Detective," she quipped. "He got himself in this predicament, wouldn't you agree?"

"I do agree, but there may be some others that helped to get him into this predicament as well," he explained. "I want to make sure you have everything you need to know to make a decision before he's put away for life. Judges' hands will be tied. They won't be able to stop it. There is no discretion. That is built into the law."

"I thought I heard that you retired, Braun," she said.

"This was supposed to be my last day."

"Looks like you picked your last day of work to go soft on me," Thomas laughed out loud. "From what I hear around this office, being soft is not your reputation."

"Yeah, I suppose reputations are only half-truths."

"I agree," she replied. "And the reputations of legends are probably even less than that."

"That is something I wouldn't know much about," he replied. "What will it take for this kid?"

"I'm going to take a good hard look at his case. I need to research his most recent history. I do not trust those print-outs. Having said that, I believe it will take two things," she lectured with a legal edge. "One: the kid needs some straight up luck to fall his way. And two: he is probably going to have to point you in the direction of a dead body to get out of this one. So, where I sit right now his luck doesn't seem to be holding up. And, the chances of him handing you a dead body is pretty fricking slim. Wouldn't you agree?"

"I'm not done talking to him," Braun shot back. "Something went on at the Weaver farm. I have no clue yet what that is. But my gut tells me to let him go at his own pace. There is something he wants to tell me."

"Looks like you aren't retiring today," Ms. Thomas snickered out loud. "Cops and their hunches." She hung up the phone.

Detective Braun lowered the phone to his waist, staring at it like he didn't know what to make of this new young prosecutor. He placed the phone onto the cradle and tried to figure out how he would explain the call to Jacob. Or if he should at all. At this point, Catherine Thomas had very little empathy for Jacob Weaver.

BRAUN WALKED BACK INTO the interview room. Jacob had laid his head down on his arms, which were resting on the table. Braun thought Jacob had fallen asleep. Jacob lifted his head and stretched, then took a sip of his coffee. It was too hot, so he grabbed the glass of water and poured a little into his coffee cup to cool it off. Braun sat down and pressed the record button once again. He shifted his notepad and pen, which was more of an unintentional OCD moment, as if he were creating space for his thoughts to settle. There was always the need for extemporaneous note-taking, which helped him look back. Braun didn't trust his old tape recorder. Blank spots, scratchy voices and whispers taught Braun to trust recorders only so far. He was still absorbing the phone call with the prosecutor. Jacob could see the distance in Braun's eyes. Thoughts were bouncing around inside his head like a pinball machine.

"What's happening?" Jacob wondered. "Is there something I should know?"

"Nothing new. Not yet. When I hear something concrete about your charges, you will be the first to know." Braun picked up his pen and began clicking the cam device. Incessantly. This did not help with Jacob's anxiety. His situation was deteriorating.

Braun knew he needed to keep Jacob's attention on his past and back on the Weaver farm. Jacob was still trying to size Braun up, since he still had a bad taste in his mouth over the runaway debacle all those years ago. Time was not a commodity that Jacob could afford any longer. Prison waited. His revelation about his grandfather's abuse, the silo as a symbol of control and retribution, obviously changed something within Jacob's psyche. One question remained for Braun. What sort of impact would this have on Ms. Thomas' decision? She may scoff at Jacob's disclosures.

In most criminal cases, empathy for the defendant is quite limited. Being a victim of abuse, or harsh discipline, may not sway the prosecutor one iota. Braun knew it, but letting Jacob open up further may illuminate more sins of the past. His grandfather's abuse forced Detective Braun to consider the fact that if this man would laugh at his grandson's crippling fear, there had to be more mistreatment in this family's history. Still, Braun needed more than just anecdotes. Just stories. He needed evidence. Braun needed to push Jacob further into his secret world. *There is something more tragic that has happened on the Weaver farm,* Braun thought to himself.

"Tell me more about your grandfather, Jacob," Braun pressed. "You said something about the tough work he made you do as a kid. What do you mean by that?"

"This may sound insignificant, but I have one story that explains how he was."

Braun sat in silence. Waiting.

"I was only ten years old and Grandpa had me trying to catch a chicken in the pen. He wanted chicken for dinner. I had a hard time catching one. I was too slow. Too little. Too scared, to be honest. "

"Scared?"

"Of the chicken. I was scared of the damn chicken. I was ten years old and those chickens run around, squawking, and whooping and hollering. They don't want to be caught."

"I see. Go on."

"'Grab the goddamn chicken, Jake. Jesus Christ it's just a chicken for God's sake.' That's what Grandpa kept hollering at me. He was scarier than the fucking chickens."

"So, even at ten years old, you knew what he wanted the chicken for?"

"Deep down I think that was part of the problem," Jacob confessed. "I was convinced the chickens knew why I was trying to catch them. But they weren't that smart. They just squawk, because they are scared of people running at them. Chasing them. Trying to grab ahold of them. I don't know if they know they're going to be killed."

"So, what happened?"

"I never did catch one. So, Grandpa got ahold of one for me. I'm sure to teach me another lesson. Just like the silo. He was pissed off now."

"You watched him kill it?"

"You're getting ahead of the story."

Braun nodded. He remained quiet and let Jacob continue.

"Like I said, I wasn't able to catch the goddamn chicken," he repeated. "So, Grandpa snatched one up by the legs."

"Was he pissed off at you still because you didn't catch one?"

"It isn't so much about being pissed at me. Grandpa was always disappointed in me. With Grandpa it was always disappointment. I don't think he knew what it was like to be ten years old, knowing this chicken was about to be killed. By me. But I didn't want to kill it. It wasn't my choice. I'm sure when he was ten, he was doing all kinds of things on the farm that never bothered him at all. That was a different time. Kids were different back then. Stuff like that had to be done."

"I think I know what happened to the chicken."

"After Grandpa caught it, he told me to come over next to him. He said he was going to teach me how to prepare the chicken for Grandma."

"Prepare it?"

"He had a two-by-four piece of wood lying on the ground. About two feet long. He told me to place the two-by-four over the back of the chicken's neck, grab the chicken by both legs and then stand on each end of the two-by-four."

"I think I see where this is going."

"Grandpa said with all my weight on the piece of wood, and the chicken's neck pinned tightly under that piece of wood, I needed to jerk its legs straight up with all my might."

"Did you do it?"

"I did," Jacob said, "but, not with any conviction."

"Conviction?"

"I knew that Grandpa wanted me to pull so hard the chicken's head would snap off. That was obvious."

"But it didn't work?"

"Like I said, I showed no conviction. I hesitated as I was pulling up, because I didn't want to feel his head come off. A ten-year-old without conviction to tear a chicken's head off? Is that really all that unusual?"

"I'd say no."

"Grandpa thought so."

"What happened?"

"I tightly gripped both the chicken's ankles. If they even have ankles. Shit, I don't know. Legs, I guess. I jerked upwards toward the sky. Like he told me to do. Both my feet came off the ends of the two-by-four. I fell hard backwards and let go of both feet. The chicken's feet, I mean."

"And you dropped it?"

"Sure. I was ten."

"I'm empathetic to how old you were."

"And the chicken took off running. But there was a terrible problem," Jacob winced from the memory. "The chicken ran around in circles. Confused. Stunned and disoriented."

"You must have been scared."

"I was scared because the chicken's neck was now about four inches longer than before I jerked on his legs. I did the job half-way."

"What did your grandpa say?"

"He told me I did a half-ass job. Like he always said. He was disappointed, of course. While he was laughing, by the way. He said I was scared of a little chicken and now he was going to have to do it. Told me when he was ten, he always prepared the chickens for dinner. Grandpa always loved to compare himself to me when he was young. How he was braver than me. Worked harder. Made him feel good."

"What happened to the chicken?"

"He walked over and grabbed the chicken by his long wobbly neck, lifted it up high in the air and quickly jerked the chicken in a fast circular motion." Jacob stood up from his chair and lifted his hand high in the air, mimicking his grandpa. "Snapped his head right off. Chicken dropped to the ground. Then, he handed me the headless, bleeding body."

"What did he say?"

"'Take this to Grandma. She will pluck it. We're having chicken for dinner.'"

"That's a helluva story."

"Grandpa smiled right through the whole ordeal," he remembered. "His laugh was as frightening as the incident. Do you think I wanted to eat that fucking long-necked chicken for dinner?"

"No, because you were ten years old and stuff like that sticks in the mind of a ten-year-old."

"Try telling that to my grandpa."

"What about your grandma?"

"What about her?"

"How did she deal with the situation? With your grandpa, I mean."

"Basically, ignored him," he said.

"What did she do with the chicken?"

"Plucked it."

"Just sat there and plucked it?"

"Well, she had to boil the chicken first to loosen the feathers. Then she started plucking it," he described. "The water was already at full boil when I got in the kitchen. She'd been watching out the window. Probably laughing at me too. She knew exactly how chickens were prepared. No surprise to her. She boiled and plucked that chicken faster than you could imagine. Done it hundreds of times."

"This has stuck in your brain? Like the silo incident?"

"Of course. You try to block it out. By the time Grandma called me back inside for dinner, that chicken was just like all the rest we ever had," he said. "She would always say, 'City folk think chickens come wrapped up in plastic from the grocery store cooler. They don't think about what happens to the thing before it makes it there.'"

Braun understood Jacob's childhood was unusual, but abusive? He hadn't quite got there yet. Who was he to say how it impacted Jacob?

It didn't matter what Braun thought. The fact was Prosecutor Thomas held all the cards. It would be her decision. Yet, he still felt a certain amount of empathy for Jacob. Braun typically didn't expend this sort of emotional baggage on routine interviews. Was this an odd mixture of retirement sentimentality and simple empathy? Detective Braun felt an unexplainable guilt for Jacob's plight, but he wasn't sure why. Perhaps, Jacob was the type of person that naturally drew you in. He was simplistic in demeanor, exuding a fragile temperament. Braun was used to protecting the weak, but typically it was the victims in his cases, and not the defendants. Braun realized, to a certain degree, he was similar as a young man. That is, until his timidity was severely tested when dropped into the unforgiving jungles of Vietnam.

FOUR

DETECTIVE BRAUN WAS UNABLE to shake Jacob's long held assertion that he had let him down when he was a juvenile runaway. It was hard to admit that he didn't remember the incident Jacob so clearly recalled. Those days were such a volatile time for Braun. Vietnam had done much more damage than he was willing to acknowledge to himself. Memories had been buried, and if not successfully buried, they were psychologically readjusted, reimagined, and justified to make his past feel less agonizing. Guilt was a ruthless enemy. He struggled for so long to forget. Now it was difficult to remember.

"Would you say you hated your grandfather?" Braun tested the boundaries of Jacob's emotions.

"Hate is a strong word."

"But he was abusive toward you." Braun was direct. "You have a tremendous amount of anger toward him, and I'm not saying that it isn't well-founded. But I can't help but believe there is something you need to tell me about him. You are hesitant. Even afraid. Tell me what is going on. Tell me what really happened on that farm. There is something more than just killing chickens and being put in the silo. What is it that still haunts you?"

"The thought of how he died."

"His death?"

"Yes. His death."

"Death certainly has a way of making people reconsider their past. Rethink their connections with people. Especially those you are supposed to be able to rely on and receive support from."

"My grandfather's death was curious."

Braun squinted. Curious was an odd way of putting it. His confusion was obvious to Jacob. He grasped his pen and wrote down that single word. *Curious.*

"I've never heard anyone refer to someone's death as curious. Are you saying his death was suspicious?"

"Yes. Only to me…apparently," he said. "No one else questioned it."

"How do people think he died?"

"Cancer. That's what they say."

"Why the suspicion then? You don't feel like he died from cancer?"

"He did have cancer. Of the colon," he explained, "but, he was recovering from surgery. That is what I was told. He went through a period of intense pain. Morphine was helping him deal with it."

"That is a powerful drug. He must have been miserable."

"He was a miserable man," he reminded Braun. "Telling the difference between the pain and his downright shitty attitude toward life was difficult. Grandma was tired of it."

"How tired?"

"Tired enough to want to be done with it."

"What are you implying?"

"I believe my grandmother saw an opportunity."

Braun scratched a quick note on his pad. *Opportunity* was an important element of crime.

"To take care of the problem," Jacob implied.

It was as if Jacob needed Braun to speak the words for him. He relied on others so much in his life, he hoped Braun would guide him down this unfamiliar path. Jacob would only nibble around the edges of an accusation.

Braun tried to navigate Jacob's vague description of events. He temporarily sat back in his chair and looked straight at him and didn't say a word. He just stared. Trying to understand who was sitting across from him. Braun's silence told Jacob that he needed to push past his ambiguous revelations. That he was going to have to be the one that told his own story. Braun opened both palms of his hands, as if to say, *what are you trying to tell me, Jacob? Just say the words.*

"This was Grandma's only chance."

"A chance to get rid of the problem? Is that what you are alluding to? Your grandpa was the problem? Her problem?"

"Let's just say, my grandmother was in control of the morphine," he said. "He trusted her. He was not in any condition to understand what was going on. She ruled the roost. When she said he was due for his morphine he never questioned it. He took it. He didn't know. He wasn't all there. He had to trust her."

"So, his life was totally in her hands?"

"It was completely in her hands," he answered, "and she took advantage of that control."

Detective Braun was walking a fine line between actively listening and provoking the words he needed to hear. He wanted Jacob to tell him exactly what happened to his grandfather, but in his own words. In his own time. Jacob was too elusive, but the word murder was hanging off the tip of his tongue. He was bogged down in the past. It was clearly too difficult for him to speak the exact words. He did not want to disparage his grandmother in any way, but he was alluding to her culpability in his grandfather's death. *Why won't he just come right out and say it? Is it the overwhelming guilt of feeling like a snitch?*

"She gave him an overdose of morphine? Intentionally?" Braun led. "Is that what you are telling me?"

"No doubt in my mind," he finally admitted.

"She intentionally killed her husband?"

"She had to have."

"You sound sympathetic to the man you hated."

"It is not about hate, Detective. I'm trying to explain, but it's very difficult to reconcile all my feelings. It's so goddamn confusing. It's not so easy to blame my grandmother for such a terrible crime."

Braun could sense Jacob's emotional conundrum. He too had acquiesced to so many questionable experiences in his own past. A sense of understanding was beginning to set in. Braun had rationalized the men he had killed in battle. They were the enemy, after all. He hated them, right? So, why the pain? Why the guilt? He understood Jacob's plight. Why did Jacob hurt over the death of a man that terrorized him so? How does the mind choose such divergent paths? Braun was beginning to question everything he had learned about extracting the truth from people.

"No man should be killed when he is helpless and dependent on the compassion of others. I can't help the fact he was an asshole. I can't change the fact he was not a good human being. I could list a thousand reasons why I should have hated the man, but no one, not even him, should be killed. Especially, by someone who wielded complete control over whether he lived or died."

Jacob was projecting now. As a youth trying to escape the hard work and mental torture of this very man. A runaway with nowhere to run. As a young man now, himself, he was trying to come to terms with a possible life in prison. All of this was creating barriers to the truth, but should have been removing those barriers instead. Jacob was obsessed with keeping his secrets buried.

"Are you saying your grandmother murdered your grandfather?"

"I will not use words like murder. There's too much pain connected to that word," he reasoned. "Emotions. Motives. Justifications. It's all so damn complicated."

"Was it murder?"

"Words like murder are for you and the prosecutor. Not people like me."

"I get what you're saying, Jacob," Braun said, "but, I won't be your mouthpiece."

"What was going on in my grandmother's mind? What sort of hatred builds up over the years? What drove her to make that final decision? Was it just opportunity? Whatever it was, I just cannot bring myself to call my grandmother a murderer."

"Your grandmother is gone," Braun reminded.

Jacob sat quietly, looking down at his hands, as if he was holding tightly onto his grandmother's reputation. Was it time to release his grip?

"You never told me how she died," Braun wondered.

"She had a bad heart. Natural causes."

"How long did she live after your grandfather passed?"

"I love how you ask that question, Detective, right after I described to you how he was drugged by my grandmother. How he passed. How he passed? I can't say the words...he just passed. That is not right. It sounds too innocent. His death was no accident."

"I understand where you're coming from," Braun said, "but before I accuse anyone of murder, I need some corroborating evidence. I can't assume she murdered him, just because you're so sure of it. Where's the evidence? She's not here to defend herself."

"Evidence? Really? That's something you may never get."

"I may not. You're correct," he agreed, "but there is not going to be a prosecution of your grandmother, anyway. She is gone. Dead. You are going to need evidence to help yourself out of this terrible mess you're in. A lot of people would say just about anything they need to say to get out of hot water. You are looking at life in prison."

"But I wouldn't denigrate the memory of my grandmother if I wasn't telling the truth," he argued. "She never did anything to harm me."

"That's clear to me, but the question the prosecutor is going to ask, is whether or not you would create a story of murder to keep yourself from going to prison for life. She needs to be convinced you're not lying. Your word alone will not cut it."

"And hurt my grandmother's name?"

"She is dead, Jacob. She can't be held accountable, if she in fact murdered him," he repeated. "The prosecutor doesn't care about upholding her name."

"This is fucking nuts!" Jacob shouted. "Why am I even telling you what I know?"

"Does anyone else know about this?"

"Just my aunt Rose."

"How do you know that?" he asked. "Did she tell you that she knows?"

"She didn't have to tell me."

Braun stood and turned his back on Jacob, showing his frustration. He was rubbing the nape of his neck. Pacing. Thinking. Using his body language to get Jacob to wake up.

"I was coming home from college for the summer," he explained. "Truth be told, I was planning on quitting school, so I wasn't in a great mood. On top of it, Grandpa had been really sick. He already had his surgery. I thought he was on the mend. I knew he had suffered with a lot of pain. That was no secret."

"So, you witnessed something?"

"I had just come through the front door of the farmhouse. I knew something was going on. Serious shit. Things just didn't feel right in the house. My aunt Rose must have heard me come through the door, because she came out of Grandpa's room and quickly shut the door behind her."

"What made you think something awful had happened to him?"

"It was how my aunt looked at me when she saw me standing in the front hallway. I knew something was terribly wrong," he said. "Grandma was still in the room with him. My aunt said, 'Don't go in there.'"

"What did you do?"

"I didn't go in," he said. "I did exactly what my aunt told me. Like always. She was on top of everything as far as I was concerned. If something had happened to Grandpa, she knew exactly what to do."

"What happened next, Jacob?"

"I sat down in the hallway, outside his room and waited. After about twenty minutes, Grandma came out of the room," he said. "I asked her what in the hell was going on. She and my aunt were being secretive. Why keep it from me? What is with the strange behavior?"

"How did she look to you?"

"Her emotions never changed much," he shook his head, recalling. "She was a stoic woman. I think I told you that already. Always matter-of-fact. But she just looked down at the floor as she walked out of his room, right past me."

"She didn't say anything to you?" Braun asked. "Did she see you were there?"

"She saw me. She knew I was there," he said. "Quietly, but loud enough for me to hear, she just said, 'Don't go in. Grandpa's gone.'"

"This sounds very typical, Jacob. There is nothing unusual about what you just explained to me," Braun said. "I would expect this type of behavior in a case like this. Old people die. Old sick people die. I'm not sure what you are telling me. You didn't believe your grandmother?"

"Nothing was unusual at that very moment," Jacob went on. "It was later. Later that night. There were things to be done. You know. Call the coroner. Call the funeral home. They would come get the body. All the arrangements were made."

"By who?" Braun asked.

"My aunt Rose. She got some help from Grandma. Like, what he would want. The color of his coffin. Or urn. Whatever he wanted. Morbid stuff like that," he explained. "But my aunt did the heavy lifting, if you know what I mean. She did all the work."

"I know exactly what you mean," he replied, "but, what happened later in the evening? You implied something occurred that was unusual. Where is the evidence, Jacob? Where? Jacob? Give me something I can wrap my head around."

"I was sitting in Grandpa's den. Just chilling. Waiting for the authorities to arrive. The house was eerily quiet. It's a small room he used as a place to sit and smoke his pipe or cigars, read the paper or his farm magazines," he said. "I'm sure my aunt and Grandma didn't know I was in there. They were sitting at the dining room table, which was just one room over from where I was sitting."

"Did you hear something?"

"I could hear them talking. Maybe not every single word, but I could hear. Enough to put two and two together. I was able to put the truth of what happened together. You know, their story they put together."

"Their story?"

"Yes. Their story. The story of what they say happened. The story that would be told," he explained. "If a story would have to be told. If they were ever questioned about his death."

"Who would question his death? Why would anyone be suspicious after an old man dies from cancer? This is not helping your case, Jacob."

"The coroner, I suppose," he said. "I don't know who else. People knew he had been sick. He did just have surgery. That was no secret. He was recovering still. That was no secret. But they needed a story. Just in case."

"Why is it needed? Why the conspiracy between your aunt and Grandmother? You've lost me."

"It was Aunt Rose. She seemed to think they needed a cover story. That's what they were talking about. Their whispering convinced me that this was not an accident. You are right, Braun. They should not have needed a story. So, why did Aunt Rose want to make sure their stories matched?"

Braun made some notes as he shook his head in frustration. He knew this was weak. He knew Jacob was in trouble. Even if he was right. Even if she did kill him. Jacob was still facing a lifetime behind bars. Braun knew if Grandma was alive, she would not be prosecuted by Catherine Thomas for the death of her husband. Not on such flimsy evidence.

"I know they talked about giving him an overdose of morphine. I heard one of them say, 'I gave him a big dose of morphine.'"

"Which one was doing the talking?" Braun pressed for details, as he picked up his pen and began to write. "Who said it exactly? Who said those exact words? Without that, you have nothing."

Jacob stood and stared at the metal door. The door that kept him from freedom. "I am as sure as I can be that it was Grandma talking. She always gave Grandpa his meds. She was in charge of the morphine. My aunt kept telling my grandma to calm down."

"What else did you hear?"

"'I'll take care of it! I'll take care of it!'" he repeated. "That's what my Aunt Rose kept saying. That is another reason I believe it was my grandmother who gave him the overdose. It sounded to me like my aunt was telling her not to worry that she would fix things. You know, clean up the damn mess. She always cleaned up the messes on the farm."

"Always?"

"Yes. Always."

"Did either one of them eventually learn that you overheard their conversation?"

"My aunt suspected it. Not my grandmother, she was too distraught over what she had just done."

"Why did your aunt suspect you heard them talking?"

"Just how I looked at her, when she saw me come walking out of the den," he said. "I could tell she wondered if I heard them talking. My aunt would not have wanted me involved. You know. Keep me far away from the crime."

"What happened next, Jacob?"

"I heard my aunt go back upstairs to Grandpa's bedroom."

"Why did she go back up?"

"I don't know. To analyze the situation? To confirm her story. Their story. Figure out if everything she would say was going to fit the scene. She had to make sure the cover-up was flawless," Jacob speculated. "Like I said, she always cleaned up the messes."

"Who would ever believe that your grandmother would intentionally kill your grandfather?"

"I don't know," he said as he reflected on his grandmother's personal life at the time.

"She was very close to her church friends?" Braun pondered, "but, confessing to murder is a serious thing to do. Telling a friend, even a close friend, does not sound like something she'd do."

"She hid the truth of her life with my grandpa, from those same people."

"If she kept this a secret, and never told anyone at the church, then only one person knows that she murdered him," Braun presumed.

"My aunt Rose. No one else could have known."

"She holds the key," Braun said. "The only key to corroborating your story."

"My aunt Rose would never expose my grandmother, Braun. Even if she is dead," he said. "She would definitely take the blame first."

"You think your grandmother could have lived with what she did?" Braun wondered. "Without asking someone, like her minister, for forgiveness? You said she was a religious woman."

"There would be only one way she could live with that kind of guilt."

"And how's that?"

"If my aunt told her she had to live with it. If she demanded it. If she told her she must keep the secret to protect the family name. Aunt Rose had that kind of control. Over all of us."

"We need to talk in depth about your aunt Rose, Jacob."

Jacob turned pale. Sickly. Was Braun demanding the impossible? Was Aunt Rose that intimidating? Did she hold that kind of control over Jacob? Over the entire Weaver family?"

"I need a break," Jacob demanded. "Right now."

Braun stood up and opened the door.

FIVE

DETECTIVE BRAUN KEPT Jacob's stories tucked away in the back of his mind, analyzing each as they were revealed. How could they help Jacob avoid a lifetime behind bars? Even if Prosecutor Thomas chose to regard them, would they create any formidable legal defense to the strict wording of the three strikes law? And even if it caused the court to verbalize a sense of empathy toward Jacob's predicament, would it have the legal muscle to change anything? But, the crime of murder may be able to sway a prosecutor to the contrary. The most important question in this moment: Did Jacob's grandmother murder his grandfather? And, even if it were true, how could it be corroborated? Thomas would demand an answer.

The two men sat back down to continue. Braun was interested in drawing more connections between Jacob's grandmother, and the rest of his family. Any piece of information that would prove the intentional killing of his grandfather could sway Prosecutor Thomas.

"I need to go back some years, when you were a kid. That will help me understand the Weaver family."

"I have no problem with that," he hesitated, "but I'm sure you'll feel it's quite boring."

"Like most childhoods, I suppose," Braun agreed. "Were you born here?"

"I was born in this county," he said.

"Where?"

"My grandpa's farm is just up Old Johnson Road."

"I'm somewhat familiar with that area."

"The Johnson farm butts up against our property," he said. "They have a big operation. My grandpa has a small farm compared to his."

"Have you always lived on the farm?"

"Believe it or not I was born on that farm."

Detective Braun's eyes widened. He was stunned. He leaned forward, elbows on the table. "I don't know anyone your age that wasn't born in a hospital."

"I'm told that my mom went into labor early," he said. "That's what you get for abusing drugs. My aunt, who was like a midwife, luckily, lived on the farm and was trying to deal with health issues my mother was having during the pregnancy. She delivered me by herself."

Braun was taken aback considering anyone would deliver a baby in a farmhouse, when a hospital was not that far away. Were the Weavers that separated from the outside world? Braun reminisced on the two deliveries his wife endured when they had their two children. The first was an emergency caesarean-section. The pain she suffered still troubled Braun to this day. He recalled her relentless screaming right before the doctor's decision to do an emergency C-section. The high-pitched screams shattered the evening silence that normally permeated the hospital hallways. The second birth went more smoothly, but she still needed another C-section as well. How did Jacob's aunt deal with the potential what-ifs? What would have happened to Jacob's mother if there was a medical emergency? Who could have saved her?

"That's the story I was told," Jacob said with a sense of uncertainty.

"Sounds like you were a lucky baby."

"Lucky? If you call lucky having a drunk and drug addict for a mother that ran off when I was only a few weeks old. That's the other side of the story my aunt likes to tell me."

"That's painful. Your grandmother and Aunt stepped up, I take it?"

"They did," he said. "But I had lots of problems."

"Medical problems?"

"The kind of problems a baby has who's born with a drug addiction."

Braun sat back and continued to listen.

"I was only two and a half pounds when I was born."

"You're lucky you survived."

"Am I?" he smirked. Jacob shook his head in disagreement.

Braun saw the hurt and considered the impact of that kind of birth. He gave Jacob some time. Let him take a breath.

"My grandmother and Aunt realized I was too small to carry in their arms. They were scared of dropping me. They carried me around in a shoebox. Can you believe that?"

"A shoebox?" Braun seemed dumbfounded. *How can an infant survive those odds?* Two and a half pounds. Effects from his mother's drug addiction. Jacob was a story of survival.

"It was actually a boot box. Grandpa had an old boot box from a pair of Red Wing work boots. He only wore Red Wings. Grandma folded up a kitchen towel and put it inside, then laid me inside the box. I fit perfectly."

"Whatever works, I suppose," Braun said. "That is the first time I have ever heard of that, but when you're two and a half pounds."

"All Grandpa bitched about was how I ruined his boot box," he said. "Grandma told me that story for years. Like it was my fault I was born premature. Grandpa was obsessed about keeping his boot boxes in good condition. When he paid for something, like boots, he felt like the box was as important as the boots. He was a major tight-ass when it came to money. What makes a man think that way, Detective? Worried about a boot box."

"It must be that generation. I've heard their stories. They did without for such a long time. With the depression and all. Material things did not come easy. Extra money was a luxury," Braun stated. "My parents kept a whole lot of stuff I had to get rid of after they passed. They couldn't part with anything at the time. Saved it all. Just in case. Throwing things away wasn't logical at the time. Who knew when it would come in handy?"

"I suppose so. Who am I to judge?"

"How was school for you as you grew up?" Braun asked.

"Hard."

"How so?"

"I missed so much. I was home-schooled more than going to public school. When I was there, I was bullied," he recalled. "I know that's a worn-out complaint."

"That's tough to go through, for any kid."

"I was so much smaller than everyone," he said. "Small then…small now."

"You weren't big enough to protect yourself, huh?"

"That's an understatement," he said. "Also, I didn't have many friends."

"So, you couldn't find a solid group of kids to hang out with?"

"I just couldn't fit in," he recalled. "I was a loner. It was like I was born to be. When I was at school I couldn't wait until the day ended. Some days I'd sneak out of school and walk four miles to the farm. Get home and get into my room. Being alone removed the pressure I felt."

"Your room became your refuge?"

"It did. It was a place to hide. No pressure. No stress. No obligations to my teachers, or other students. Everything came hard for me."

"So, who did you get along with?" Braun asked. "Who did you consider your friends?"

"I got along with some of the younger kids."

"How much younger?"

"Two or three years."

"How could you relate to kids that much younger than you?"

"I just could…I never thought that much about it," he said. "It seemed like I was on their level. Probably because of my size, I was viewed as younger. I didn't feel the pressure."

"You were in more control of situations with them?"

"I will admit that being in control gave me a sense of power. You know, get my way, and take control of the situations I found myself in. I couldn't do that with older kids. That was a big part of those relationships. We were not close friends, the more I think about it."

"Did you feel older than them?"

"Not really older, I just felt smarter," he recalled. "I couldn't relate to the older kids or even the kids my age. It seemed easier to be around the younger kids. Less stress."

Braun began to see the constant thread that wove through Jacob's upbringing. There was much talk about stress, being a loner and the desire to avoid confrontation. His anxiety, as a young man now, clearly derived from his upbringing.

"I thought I was supposed to hang around people. That is what society expects. That's what we are all supposed to do, right? If you don't socialize there is something wrong with you. They think you're weird."

"You wanted to be alone?" Braun asked.

Now, Braun began to understand Jacob's desire for cannabis. The high let him deal with all these issues in his life. He relied on it.

"For sure. There is no pressure when you're alone."

"Do you feel that way still? Or was that in the past?"

"Honestly, I can't tell what is what anymore," he said. "I finally learned to accept who I am. Do I love me? No. Do I hate me? No."

"You accept you."

"I accept me," Jacob grinned, recalling his past. "What are my options?"

Braun hesitated, writing some notes. He paused and let the silence saturate their space. He was trying to understand Jacob's self-doubt, and self-loathing. He had two crimes hanging over his head. They were an obstacle to freedom. Was a DUI and possession of marijuana so hard to understand? Were these the crimes that should cause a young man to spend the rest of his life in prison? Braun never considered himself a bleeding-heart, and he understood the need to deter crime, but he also knew Jacob was not the person who should be the poster child for the three strikes law. For the first time in over thirty years on the job, Braun was trying to keep someone out of prison instead of trying to put them in. He realized he was building a history of Jacob's life in his mind. It helped him understand how Jacob became this troubled young man. The DUI, the marijuana used to simply make it through the day.

One major dilemma remained. The three strikes law was not empathetic to one's psychological struggles of the past. It focused on one's criminal history. This is the reality that forced Jacob into a corner. This was the fact of the matter at hand. His situation drew a stark contrast between the so-called correctional system and the penitentiary. They were supposed to be one in the same, but were they in a case such as this? Even if behavior is corrected, the prisoner remains behind bars, with no chance of freedom. How does a two and a half-pound premature infant, grow into a young man still searching for a way to survive?

SIX

HOW DO PEOPLE ARRIVE, where they are, at any given time in their life? Braun thought about his journey, and how a large part of it was supposed to end today. Instead, he meets Jacob and is thrust into this stranger's uncontrollable fate. It was as if they were both gliding down two parallel highways, not noticing one another, when Jacob veered off course, crashing into a long-lost memory. A fate bombarded by such chaos, forced Braun to postpone the next chapter in his own pending story. Jacob seemed less concerned about his own plight than Braun. There was an aura of two existences, inadvertently intertwined by very different sets of circumstances. Two men, one older, one younger, dancing to the rhythm of unfamiliar music, of which neither one could recognize. The only comfort Jacob sensed, perhaps out of guilt, was Frank Braun's willingness to stay by his side until the last stanza concluded. Jacob reached out, in his own simple way, for more of the empathy Braun seemed willing to provide.

"You must have stories, Detective."

"None that would interest you," Braun said. "I don't have any chicken stories, if that's what you mean."

"I noticed your hands," Jacob said, pointing. "Don't suppose you want to give me the story behind those scars?"

"Not much of a story." Braun tried to misdirect Jacob, shifting the attention back onto him.

"Let me be the judge of that," he said. "If you want me to keep talking and get down to the real reason I'm in this mess, you're gonna have to do your part."

"My part? I didn't know I had a part in this."

"Of course you do. This must be a two-way street, as they say. What happened to your hands, Braun? Why the scars?"

"Fair enough."

Braun took a minute and paused, looking down at his visibly scarred hands. He didn't think much about the burns anymore. They were part of him now. Jacob was the first person in years to even notice them. Most people wouldn't want to dredge up other people's past misfortunes, but not Jacob. He was socially awkward. The scars piqued his interest, so he asked. Braun was learning quickly that this was part of Jacob's personality. Braun's badly scarred hands were a reminder of a distant past, and how truly far away from that past he had moved.

"I was six years old."

"Aha...I knew you had a childhood story in you, Detective."

"I got burned. Both hands. Up my arms."

"How did that happen? Six is pretty young to get burned. Firecrackers by any chance?"

"No. Not firecrackers," he replied. "At a birthday party for a buddy of mine."

"Birthday? He was turning six, too."

"He was turning six too," he said. "His father had chopped down a tree in the backyard. There was a big stump left. He decided to burn out the inside of it. It had burned down all the way to the ground."

"So, the outside of the stump was just a wooden shell?"

"Yes. About three foot high. We decided..."

"Who's we?" he interrupted.

"My buddy, three other boys and me," Braun explained, reluctantly.

"Don't even tell me..."

"We lined up. About fifteen feet away. Because we were planning on running and jumping over the shell of that burned out stump."

"Let me guess, you went first?"

"I went first."

"What happened?"

"I ran as fast as I could and leapt as high as I could. I needed to get over the front edge of the stump, but the toes of my tennis shoes caught the top edge and flipped me forward, hard. I went head first down inside the stump."

"Which was still burning?"

"Still burning, yes. In the bottom of that wooden shell was about four inches of hot white ash and red-hot embers. The sparks still flared up now and again."

"Hotter than hell, right Braun?"

"That goes without saying," Braun winced, as if he could still feel the heat. "Because I had flipped inside head first, I was doing a hand-stand with both hands, up past my wrists, buried under those coals and my feet were sticking out at the top of the stump's outer shell. I was stuck. Nothing I could do but hope someone would pull me out. My hands were on fire."

Jacob sat back so hard in his chair he went up on two legs and almost tipped over.

"That is some crazy shit. How did you get out? Your six-year-old buddies couldn't pull you out."

"They screamed for my mother, who was inside with all the other mothers, having coffee and talking," he said, "but, they heard the screams."

"Your mother saved you?"

"She ran out and grabbed me by the ankles. Pulled me straight up, out of the fire."

"Your mother loved you. I bet she was a good woman, your mother," he grinned. "My mother would have let me burn. Forget that. My mother wouldn't have even been at the party with the other ladies. She'd have been off partying by herself somewhere."

"That's it. That is all there is to the story."

"How bad were you burnt? You had to have gone to the hospital."

"She threw me in the front seat of our old Chevy Bel Air and rushed me to the hospital about fifteen miles away. She said I screamed all the way."

"And carried you into the emergency room?"

"She did. Third degree burns on both hands. Second degree on my arms and face."

"Jesus Christ, Detective. You can't tell," he said. "No scars on your face. That's good. Your hands, I can see the scars. You were only six years old? You said you had no stories, Braun. That is bullshit. We all have our stories."

"I don't think much about it anymore. That was a long time ago."

"Makes my chicken story sound pretty childish. I was ten. You were just six, burning up in a damn fire. I was crying like a goddamn baby over a long-neck chicken."

"We all have our own stories," Braun said. "They are all important to our lives in their own way."

"I know you mean well," he said, "but it's hard to compare getting burnt in a damn fire to Grandpa making me wring a chicken's neck."

"They are totally different. Like the silo story."

"Don't patronize me," Jacob replied, testy.

"We're here to talk about you. You are the one sitting in jail. Remember, you are facing a lot of prison time, Jacob," Braun reminded.

"The three strikes law is hanging over your head like a dark cloud."

"I'm sure this new prosecutor is itching to put me behind bars, isn't she Braun?"

Detective Braun had no response. He couldn't answer him truthfully. Even if he was able to predict the prosecutor's objective, he knew she was not about to show all her cards at this point. Jacob Weaver was an unknown entity to her. He was just a man with a criminal history. And it fit right into the three strikes statute. That possibly meant a very long time in prison. For a young man like Jacob, a death sentence.

BRAUN LEFT THE ROOM. He called the prosecutor for any updates on what was going to happen to Jacob. There had to be an arraignment put on the schedule soon. Jacob needed to go in front of a judge and have the charges explained. Braun knew Thomas could shed some light on what lay ahead, but he also knew this was not the only case she had on her plate. Her line rang.

"This is Thomas," she answered.

"It's Braun. Anything I should know about how you'll proceed with Weaver?"

"His arraignment will be tomorrow morning," she advised, "unless you pull something out of your hat and get it postponed. I was about to call you. I wanted you to know that at the arraignment he will be assigned the public defender. I assume he doesn't have any money?"

"Any decisions regarding the three strikes law?"

"Not yet," she hesitated, "but, I am considering dropping the DUI."

"Issues with probable cause?"

"Your guy blew a .06 blood alcohol on the breath test," she reminded him. "The legal limit is .08, although this guy should not be driving at .06 either. I don't doubt he was impaired. The officer reported his driving was erratic. And Weaver did fail the probable cause tests. Apparently, he couldn't walk a straight line if his life depended on it. So, I don't doubt the officer at all, but I would have rather had him blow .08 or over. Weaver cannot hold his booze, but that alone isn't a crime."

"What about the cannabis?"

"Hey, the war on drugs still rages on, Braun," she answered. "Not much I can do about the dope. The ball is in your court on that one. Come up with something today and we will take another look at it. He is going to be arraigned on a drug charge no matter what. The three strikes will hinge on the drug charge. No doubt. The judge will not be happy either."

"In ten or fifteen years all this shit will be legal."

"And when it is, the three strikes law will have screwed a whole lot of people."

Detective Braun stepped into the room next door, to view the monitor that kept watch over Jacob. This was the gadget room, for lack of a better description, where detectives were able to view the interrogation process. Make judgments on the demeanor of suspects, while they were alone with their thoughts. The camera was perfectly situated to pick up Jacob's every movement. Braun noticed how he studied the tiny, nondescript room. Looked high and low. At the walls. At the locked door. He leaned forward and looked down at the dirty tile floor. Between his feet. Jacob peered up at the corner of the ceiling, straight into the camera. He grinned. It was as if he was looking right through the camera lens, straight into Braun's eyes. He couldn't have known he was watching. Did Jacob know what he was doing? Or was he as innocent as he acted? Jacob still hid many secrets. Braun had a gut feeling about that as he reentered the room.

"Let's get back to it."

"We were discussing my exciting life," Jacob smiled. "No one has ever wanted to talk about my past so much. It's funny talking about it now."

"How so?"

"I thought that my life was completely hidden from the outside world."

"I don't understand."

"Hidden from view," he clarified. "I always believed my life was insulated from everyone on the outside of the Weaver farm fence line. Like I was in a cocoon."

Braun paused. "You don't think anyone cares about you, is that it?"

"Sort of," he replied. "I'm not sure if I think they don't care, or if they are just so engrossed in their own lives that they didn't realize I existed."

Again, Braun noticed a thread that ran through all of Jacob's memories. Feelings of isolation. The realization that the Weaver family had walled themselves off from the outside world. He tried to fit in, but found it alien to his nature.

"So, you aren't really blaming anyone for not caring anything about you?"

"How could I blame complete strangers for not taking the time to care about me?" he smirked. "You never cared much about me until today, right?"

"I see what you're getting at."

"How could you possibly know anything about me? How I got to be who I am. Where I've been. Why I am who I am today."

"Do you want more people to care about you?" Braun asked. "Is that what you are trying to tell me?"

"I don't think about it anymore. It's too late, Braun," he said. "People should have cared about me when I was younger."

"Is that when it is important?"

"Youth is the only time you can develop. I mean truly develop into who you are. Who you will be. Don't you agree with that?"

"Those are valid points."

"I heard once, and don't quote me if I'm wrong," he said, "but, I believe a person's brain develops more in the first three years of their life than the rest of their years combined. Something like that. I probably got that wrong, but it's something crazy like that. You know what I mean. Have you ever seen how a three-year-old soaks things in? They're like a damn sponge."

Braun looked into Jacob's eyes. *Does he realize the trouble he is in?*

"Do you have any kids, Detective?"

"I have two," he said. "But they're grown now. Both in their twenties."

"Boys? Girls?"

"One of each."

"I bet they're successful."

"They are healthy, and I think happy," he said. "Knock on wood, because you never know what a new day will bring."

"You never know. You're right about that," Jacob thought. "Look where drinking in the morning got me."

"You said you didn't have any siblings, right?" Braun re-affirmed.

"That's right," Jacob replied with some uncertainty. "As far as I know."

"As far as you know?"

"Who knows with my mother?" Jacob answered. "Iris was unpredictable."

"Iris? Who all lived on the farm?"

"Grandma and Grandpa. Aunt Rose. And me."

"Not your mother?" he pressed. "Not Iris?"

"I don't really consider her my mother. She was in and out of my life so much, I can't even give you a time frame when she was there on the farm with us."

"I'm not trying to stir up old memories."

"But you are, whether you are trying to or not. I expect it," he said. "Lots of things make me pissed off, so don't be surprised if you see it. No offense, Detective."

"Point taken."

"Do you really understand, or are you just saying what you think I want to hear?"

"I was going to ask you the same question," Braun responded, showing his frustration with Jacob's seeming ignorance of his own predicament. "You are asking me to trust the things you say. What is it about me that you don't trust?"

"You are a cop, Braun. My aunt taught me not to trust cops. Especially, the cop that abandoned me. I was only twelve, Detective. Now, you are trying to get to the truth about what happened," he said. "I'm waiting for the bad cop to walk in here and threaten me. Tell me I will never see the light of day. Tell me I'm going to burn in hell for the things I've done. Tell me my life is over."

"I don't play those kinds of games, Jacob," he said. "You have watched too much television. I have no reason to threaten you. I'm here to listen."

"What makes you believe I will tell you the truth now? The last time I told you the truth it made things worse for me. I was placed back on that farm, because you would not listen. You didn't have the time. Or, maybe, you were too drunk."

"I don't drink, Jacob." Braun immediately got defensive. Jacob's allegation struck a nerve. It was obvious. He felt the blood rushing to his face.

"You drank when I was twelve," Jacob vented. "I was just a kid, but I knew. I knew you didn't care about the things that happened to me. The shit going down on that farm. You were too drunk to care. You really don't remember?"

"How do you know I was drunk?" Braun leaned forward placing his elbows on the table, challenging Jacob. He was exposing Braun's most regrettable secret. "Why is that what you remember about me?"

"Because Iris was always drunk. Or high," he recalled. "My so-called mother. I learned from a very early age that adults, especially drunk adults, do not give a rat's ass about me. They worried about their next drink. You didn't stick around long that day, after dropping me off at the farm. I wanted to tell you things, but after you talked to my aunt, you decided I had nothing important to say. You didn't have the time, or motivation, to listen to a kid."

"If it makes any difference, I haven't had a drink in almost fifteen years," Braun revealed. "So, I'm listening to you now."

"It does make a difference," Jacob replied.

Braun was stunned into complete silence. His worst memories from that time in his life instantaneously jolted him back into the darkness. The psychological barriers he had built for himself, to hide from his guilt, were being broken down by one young man. A young man who faced life in prison. A young man with nothing to lose by telling the truth. Jacob was dredging up Braun's most painful secrets. He was convinced the secrets he had buried so long ago had disintegrated, along with the embarrassment and guilt, like a pile of dead autumn leaves. Braun was wrong. They haunted him still. He just didn't realize it until he met Jacob.

Braun was not able to fight off those memories, as a young soldier, after returning from Vietnam. Drinking helped him forget the blood and the death. To forget those back home, who hated him for doing his duty. Drinking to forget the day his wife took his two children and walked out of his shattered life. Leaving him with a bottle of booze in one hand and a nine-millimeter in the other. Wondering if he should. If he could. Wondering if the world would be a better place without him. His eventual recovery, of regaining relationships with his children, and the fact that he became a decorated police officer, could not seem to shake the memory of failing Jacob Weaver in that single moment in time. Jacob was right. The more he reminded Braun of his failure to help him, the more his memories were illuminated. Braun's recollection of that day was now beginning to come back to him. Right along with the guilt.

SEVEN

DETECTIVE BRAUN COULD ONLY make amends one way to the child that still lived within Jacob. The child that was ignored at the age of twelve. Braun may not ever know what Jacob wanted to tell him as a child. What really happened on the Weaver family farm? So much time had passed. So much water had passed under that proverbial bridge. What could Braun do now? He could not create a history out of whole cloth. He could only help reveal what had once existed. Reveal the facts. Jacob had committed two felonies in his late teens, and early twenties. Now, they were coming back to haunt him. Unfortunately, neither one could undo the past.

"Can you trust me now?" Braun asked. "Will you?"

"I appreciate what you're asking," he stated. "That is why I like you, Braun. You seem to tell it like it is. No bullshit. No threats. No twisting of my words."

"I listen. That's my job," he said. "One thing about listening. If you have the patience, the desire, and the respect of the person talking, listening is one of the easiest things to do."

"I think you're right," he agreed. "I lived a lifetime without people listening to me. They didn't hear a word I said. They didn't care about what I had to say. I assumed listening was just so damn hard. Nobody would take the time to do it."

"I feel like you may be talking about your grandfather again?"

"That goes without saying," he answered. "He was a lost cause when it came to listening to me. Or anyone for that matter."

"He didn't listen to your grandmother either?"

"I believe deep down he listened to her, he just ignored what she said," he remembered. "Like out of spite or something. He treated her and the church the same way. Didn't much listen to either one of them. Somewhere along the way he must have been damaged."

"How so?"

"Grandpa suffered from shell-shock, whatever that is," he said. "That's what Grandma called it. He served in WWII. The way I see it, he survived the war. But, not the coming home. He never got over all the men that died around him. She said he was never the same when he came home. I guess they just had nothing they could do for those men."

"You've heard of PTSD?"

"That's pretty well known."

"Sounds like that's what he suffered from," Braun explained, with personal knowledge. "It can change a man."

"And he came from a generation that never truly dealt with it, right?"

"I'm no psychologist, but if that is what your grandma told you, she's probably right," he agreed. "No one knows better than the spouse."

"Grandma knew about it. She just couldn't do anything about it."

"How was she able to handle it?" Braun asked. "After all she did spend her entire life with the man."

"She did," he said. "But, how much of her dedication came from a false sense of duty?"

"What do you mean?"

"You know, until death us do part. All that bullshit."

"I'm sure that's not how she saw things."

"Why do old people always stick it out?" he asked. "Where do they get that sense of obligation? He was a terrible prick, Detective. She could have had a better life."

"Where would she have gone?"

"That's a good question," he said, "but, she could have found a way out. Could have had her own life."

"Did you ever see him hurt her?"

"No…never…and I don't think he ever would have," he said, "but, I think he did something worse."

"The neglect?"

"Neglect is worse," he stated. "She was invisible to him. I don't know if he ignored her intentionally, or if his mental health issues caused him to be inside this shell he couldn't crawl out of. I just don't have the insight to know what in the hell was going on inside his mind. He was a tortured man. I felt that."

"How did your grandmother handle it?"

"She lived her own life. She did her own thing. She worked on the farmhouse. Worked at the church, and volunteered when she was able. She helped take care of me. I think she spent her time quietly surviving."

"She never lashed out?"

"Not in the way I think you're assuming."

"I didn't mean to assume anything. I just wondered how she held up without showing her anger. She had to be an angry woman."

"If she was an angry woman, she had a great way of hiding it," he recalled. "She was a very stoic woman. I thought it was the Pennsylvania Dutch in her. Always seemed calm. She was a tough old gal."

"Were they both of German heritage?"

"I would say German and then Grandpa would correct me. He'd say, 'We are Pennsylvania Dutch,'" he recalled, shaking his head. "Do I know the difference?"

"Did your grandpa ever knock you around?" Braun asked. "When he disciplined you, I mean."

"No, not really," he said. "Or I was just used to it? But what was worse for me was the fact he pretended I didn't exist. No kid wants that. I was just someone that lived on the farm. He spoke few words to me. I really don't know for sure why. Maybe he was that broken."

Detective Braun found himself within a situation he had never been, since he became a detective. He was not talking to Jacob like a cop. He was not interviewing or interrogating him. Braun thought to himself that he was not trained for this type of interaction. There was no flow or pattern to the interview. He was speaking to Jacob without following a step-by-step method of extracting information. Jacob would open up, eventually. Braun could feel it, but it would be at his own pace.

"How did your mother and her sister get along?"

"Like fire and ice. Or like oil and water. Whatever that old saying is," he stated. "I'm trying to tell you they didn't get along."

"Why did you think that?"

"They could be cordial, but my aunt hated my mother's behavior," he said. "Saw her as childish and self-serving, like the world revolved around her. That pissed my aunt off."

"And your aunt was just the opposite?"

"My aunt was more like my grandmother. Focused on protecting the family name," he said. "She'd do anything for the family."

"Anything?" Braun questioned. "Doing anything for a family member is beyond dedication. That is real loyalty"

"That's my aunt Rose."

"Was she a homebody?"

"That's an understatement," he answered, raising his eyebrows. "She was like a recluse, to be more accurate. There was a lot to do on the farm. Grandpa wouldn't, or couldn't, do it all. There were chores. They had to get done. Nobody argued about it. Nobody challenged the unwritten rules. They just did what they thought was within their realm. My aunt was in charge."

"But, not your mother?"

"Oh no, no. Not Iris. That kind of work was way beneath her," he sarcastically explained. "That was another reason my aunt couldn't stand her. That was the impression I had of those two and how they got along."

"I know it is unusual, but did you ever see them fight? Physically?" he asked. "Did either of them get violent with the other?"

"I remember a few stand-offs where I thought they were going to get into some hair-pulling, but I never witnessed it myself. I got the impression when they were girls, they probably got violent with each other. How can I say for sure? I wasn't around to see it with my own eyes. It's just a guess, Detective."

"But you heard them argue?"

"When my mom was around, they were always arguing," he said. "So, I assume it was most of the time. Because, my mom wasn't around much."

"Who is older?"

"Aunt Rose."

"Who ran the farmhouse?"

"What do you mean by that?"

"Who was in charge around the house? Your grandma?"

"No. I'd say Aunt Rose. In certain ways they were much alike. Not so much in other ways. I suppose like any time there is a mother daughter comparison. You see some things that are alike and then you find things that aren't."

"Anything you can pinpoint?"

"My aunt would have been more apt to act on things she said she was going to do," he said. "Grandma may have had the exact same opinion about things, but probably wouldn't have acted on it."

"Grandma was all talk and no action is that it?"

"I'm not trying to paint her as a woman that shot her mouth off, who didn't stand by what she said," he explained. "It's just that my aunt was more impulsive and would have reacted to things more quickly. Maybe that's just because she is younger and from a different generation. My aunt was more about taking action. Solving things that she thought were a problem. Not letting it fester and turn into something worse. It's hard to explain."

Braun paused for a moment, thinking of Aunt Rose's role on the farm. He wrote some notes. A theme was developing around Aunt Rose's need to control everything. She controlled the farm, house, her parents and Iris and Jacob. She saw herself as a problem solver. She cleaned up the messes, as Jacob described.

"Did you have brothers or sisters, Detective?"

"One sister and a brother."

"Younger?"

"Yes, younger than me."

"I knew it. I can just tell by your way that you are the oldest."

Braun sat and waited for Jacob's analysis. He knew it was coming.

"You seem composed. You're in control, if you know what I mean."

"I don't know the psychology behind sibling order of rank."

"You seem self-confident. I get the feeling it would be hard to shake you, Braun," he said, his eyes squinting with more questions. A coy grin followed. Hoping he had correctly guessed the personality of Braun. "I'm not sure how much your parents were able to control you. You were somewhat of a rebel, weren't you? Were you a soldier?"

"I was a Marine."

"Where?"

"Vietnam."

"You saw a lot of killing?"

"I saw killing."

"And you killed people?"

"I killed the enemy."

"That's tough on a man, even when it's the enemy."

"It can change a man."

"You understand my grandpa, don't you?" he asked. "When I was describing my grandpa, you understood why he was the way he was?"

"I could relate, somewhat, to what he went through. The description of your grandfather sounded familiar."

"Are you cold to death?" he asked. "Calloused? I suppose between war and police work you must be hardened toward death and all the negative shit out in the world."

"If I am it's not intentional," he replied. "I try not to be, but it does happen."

"What if I am not what I seem, Detective?" he asked. "What if I'm not the kind of person that I appear to be?"

"It takes a long time to learn about people," Braun answered. "I don't expect to know anyone after the first time I meet them. Sometimes you think you know someone and even after a lifetime they still surprise you. It happens. There's not much you can do about it. Part of life."

"What if you never figure me out?"

"That's not what I'm trying to do," he said. "You have something to tell me, Jacob. I'm still not exactly sure what it is, but I'm here til I find out."

"Fair enough," he said. "You're a persistent man. I'm learning that quickly, Braun."

"Why talk to me? Why not someone else?" Braun asked. "Is it because of the runaway incident all those years ago?"

"I saw the article."

"What article?"

"The one in the local paper. It was on the front page two days ago. Someone wrote about your career and upcoming retirement."

"I haven't even read that article myself," Braun admitted. "Quite frankly, I was leery about reading it. I wasn't sure if they would hype my career since I'm leaving. They have a tendency to do that sort of thing. It can be a little embarrassing."

"There's no reason to be embarrassed. It was a good article," he replied. "You had a successful career. It's worth writing about. They painted a picture of you that made me feel safe. I thought I could talk to you and you'd be straight with me. That's just the gut feeling I got. It rustled up some old memories. I wanted to give you a second chance. Like I want to be given."

"I'm not sure I can live up to a newspaper article," Braun confessed. "Now, let's get back to your aunt Rose."

EDUCATED GUESSES WOULD only lead a detective to go in a certain direction, but it is not evidence. If Aunt Rose corroborated Jacob's version of events, this would surely bolster his recollection of what he believed happened all those years ago. When all is said and done, Jacob may be exactly right about what transpired. Perhaps his grandmother did give his grandfather an overdose of morphine. This, in fact, may have ended his life. But, premeditated? Murder? Is that what Braun thought happened to Mr. Weaver? Was this a woman that could kill? How easy to say intentional instead of accidental, with no evidence that proves his story. This wasn't going to cut it, and Braun was sure of it. This is not what Thomas was talking about when she said to bring her something serious. He knew she expected something legally serious, something without all the baggage of ambiguity. The justice system owed Jacob Weaver nothing. Jacob was trapped. Braun knew it. He saw the emptiness in Jacob's eyes. He heard the loneliness in his voice. He wanted to talk about anything but his own predicament. Braun had to steer Jacob in another direction. He had to focus on the relationship between Iris and Rose. The volatility. The anger. Jacob described the family's relationship with Iris as nothing short of a festering wound.

EIGHT

"I NEED TO KNOW MORE about Iris," Braun said. "I know it's a sore subject, but the relationship you had with her was troubling."

"Troubling? That's one way of putting it," he answered with a smirk. "She was a bad influence on me for fifteen years."

"Fifteen years?" Braun squinted with confusion.

"That's when she took off. For good."

"I thought you said she was in and out of your life."

"She was," he explained, "until I was fifteen years old. That was the last time she left the farm. I never saw her again."

"You have not seen your mother since you were fifteen?" Braun was clearly stunned. He leaned back and locked his fingers behind his head. This didn't sound possible.

"I haven't."

"How old are you now?"

"I'm twenty-nine."

"You have not seen or heard from your mother in almost fourteen years?" Braun probed in disbelief. "Has anyone in your family ever told you why? Usually there is some communication between family members. Your grandma, maybe? Your aunt? Someone knows something. Someone has spoken to her."

"Nothing. Absolutely nothing," he repeated. "Most people would consider that extremely unusual, but you didn't know Iris. She would take off for weeks. Even months at a time. I did not see her for almost a year when I was thirteen. Not a word."

"Where did you think she was?"

"Out of sight. Out of mind," Jacob said. "Maybe she was in jail? I assumed she was living down south. Seeing her again was just a roll of the dice."

"How long would she stay on the farm when she did show up?"

"Long enough to get money. Or long enough to get bored. Whichever came first."

"And that usually took days, or weeks?"

"Weeks usually," he said. "Even months sometimes, if she felt she had nowhere else to go."

"What did your grandma and your aunt think of her behavior?"

"They thought it was despicable," he recalled. "They didn't approve. But, what could they do about it? They tried shaming her into straightening out. They used the guilt trip on her. Grandpa always ended up giving her money. Probably wasn't much, but enough to cause her to take off again. He always gave in to her. I don't know why. Maybe he gave her money so she would leave. Honestly, I was too young to remember what was going on."

"Do you believe your mother is still alive?" Braun asked. "Fourteen years is a very long time to be gone missing, Jacob, unless, she started a whole new life somewhere. In most cases like this, she would be considered deceased."

"Even if there is no body?"

"Even if there is no body," he explained. "Too much time has passed."

"Do I really care?" His deep resentment was palpable. "Whether she is dead or alive, she has been dead to me for many years now. How could she not be? Iris abandoned me when I needed her most. Even if she wasn't much of a parent. When you're a child, you accept your mother, no matter what. Until you grow up. Things change. There wasn't a single day that I can remember Iris ever acting like my mother."

"And you mean that literally? Or, could this be your anger finally coming out? No one would blame you."

"I mean it literally," he said. "I don't remember Iris ever holding me on her lap. I don't remember her ever reading to me or putting me to bed. I cannot honestly remember Iris ever kissing me goodnight. It just never happened, Detective. Sounds hard to believe, I know, but there are people like her out in this world."

"There are. You shouldn't have had to go through that," Braun agreed. "Did your grandmother or Aunt Rose step into her role?"

"To a certain point, yes," he said. "My grandma acted like a grandma. My aunt Rose acted like a mother to me. Like my real mother. When you're a kid you take love from wherever you can get it, right? My aunt Rose gladly gave it and I gladly took it."

Something did not smell right. It stunk, as a matter of fact. Braun had seen a lot in his career, but a mother missing for all those years? And the woman's sister stepping into the role of mother, with such purpose? *She gladly gave it and I gladly took it.* Odd. Very odd.

"Jacob, somebody did something right by you," he complimented.

"I don't know what you mean," Jacob replied, scrunching his eyebrows.

"Raising you," he clarified. "You sound like a young man that is well-educated. You're articulate. You seem very bright to me."

"You aren't the only one that believes the stereotype that poor farmers are stupid hicks. We're uneducated rubes, is that it?" he laughed. "I done read books, Detective. I's smarter than yawl think."

Jacob laughed at his misguided impression of the stereotypical dumb hillbilly. "Farmers have often been looked down upon by elitist. You know, we're those country bumpkins living out in the backwoods."

"I didn't mean to imply anything," Braun explained. "I'm just telling you what I see in you. It's a compliment. Someone influenced the way you think."

"My aunt Rose," he said. "She was an avid reader. And I do mean obsessive. You'll find every classic novel you can think of strewn about the farmhouse."

"I take it, she made you read?"

"No television. When I was young, she was a librarian at the local library. That was all I ever knew her to do, other than taking care of the farm. She brought home more books than you can imagine. I don't know if she was stealing them, or borrowing them, but all I know is that we have hundreds. All the classics. Not just any book off the shelf."

"Why did she make you read so much?"

"Because she told me that school wouldn't give me the education these books would give me," he recalled. "About life, I mean. She wasn't big on public school. She told me everything I needed to know about life was documented inside those books."

"Your aunt may have been onto something."

"I'm serious, Braun. I was reading Faulkner before I was twelve. You know his works, *The Sound and the Fury*, *Light in August*. I have read all his stuff. Have you read anything by Steinbeck? She made me read *The Grapes of Wrath* by the time I was thirteen. Aunt Rose would tell me if I ever thought times were rough, just read Steinbeck.

She was right. She knew these authors inside and out. I read authors like Hemingway...Fitzgerald. I read Mark Twain, because he took me to other places. Familiar places. We don't live all that far from the Mississippi river. Can you believe that? The river Twain was writing about is not far from this farm. I read Orwell's *Animal Farm* in my early teens. Not because I lived on a farm either. That's no children's book, Detective. It's a good lesson for adults that find it necessary to control others. It taught me about fairness. About equality. About freedom. My aunt Rose should have taken Orwell more seriously. You're like an old classic, Braun. Maybe all these novels led me to a man like you."

"I'm not sure about that, but if it wasn't for the DUI and your possession of weed, I don't think we would have ever crossed paths again."

"That's funny," Jacob smiled. "Who would have thought a guy like you had such a good sense of humor?"

"You said your aunt Rose was controlling," Braun reiterated. "How controlling?"

"She controlled my whole life," he admitted, as he thought back. "In a sense, I was a prisoner on that farm. She would tell me it was for my own good. That it was all out of love. To protect me from the outside world. She saw the outside world as her enemy."

"Aunt Rose never had any children of her own?" Braun asked.

"She couldn't. I was her child. In her heart. In her mind. And that was how she treated me."

Detective Braun began to see a clear picture developing in his mind's eye. A picture of control being painted, subtly, perhaps not intentionally, by Jacob. Aunt Rose controlled her parents, her sister, the Weaver family farm, and especially Jacob. Was the control out of love, if that was possible, or out of an internal desire for the control itself? Braun needed to dig further. He scanned some of his notes.

"I want to get back to your mother, Jacob. Your biological mother. Why do you remember so clearly that you were fifteen when she left for good? Shouldn't her leaving just have been another one of those typical instances? Why was this time different?"

"This time stood out, because it was one time she made it clear that she would be coming back," he said. "It sticks in my mind. Maybe it was just talk, trying to make herself look responsible. I don't know, but she had never taken the time to tell me before. She just disappeared."

"She told you, specifically, or told everyone?"

"It wasn't just me. They were arguing about it. Again. That's why I remember."

"Who was arguing?"

"Iris and Aunt Rose."

"What was going on in your life at the time that makes this incident stand out?" Braun pushed him to remember.

"I know because I was just learning to drive," he said. "I was turning sixteen. I remember that clearly, because my birthday meant freedom. You know, *Animal Farm*. Getting out. Running my own life. I was approaching that age when I could be free to go. Even though I didn't have a car at the time. There was still a sense of getting out, in my head anyway. I could sense the feeling of freedom. I had never felt that before. The day was coming."

"So, you watched Iris leave?" Braun re-checked.

Before Jacob could answer, there was a knock on the interview room door.

"Hold your thought, Jacob."

Detective Braun stood and went to the door. It was the desk sergeant. He handed Braun a small stack of computer print-outs.

"Here are those searches you requested," the sergeant said. Braun shut the door and returned to the table. He laid the paperwork down and looked back at Jacob. "Sorry Jacob. Go on."

Braun was scanning some of the print-outs on the table as Jacob spoke. His eyes landed on something important. He focused on one specific paragraph in the document.

"I saw her leave the farm," he said.

Braun looked up and watched Jacob's eyes closely. He hesitated and thought back on the actual event. Jacob was so young. It was so long ago.

"Let me think for just minute. I was actually leaving the farm that day, too. Iris did say to me, 'See you the next time I come back.' It was usually just talk. Just bullshit that made her feel good. I knew that. I was used to the lies. So, I left the farm with a friend of mine."

"Who with?"

"It was a kid down the way. He lived on a farm just two miles up Old Johnson Road. We got along okay and hung out."

"Were you close friends?"

"Not really, but he could drive and his dad let him drive one of the work trucks on the farm. It was something to do. Someone to hang out with."

"So, on that very day you actually left the farm before Iris left the farm?"

"That's probably true, but I'm sure she was about to leave right after me," he said. "And as you can see, she left shortly after I did. And here we are fourteen years later and she's still gone."

"Was she with the man you referred to as your step-father?"

"Wyatt? No, he wasn't there. I can't say where he was, but Iris was alone."

"Did you always call your mom, Iris?"

"I never thought that much about it. Why?"

"It seems odd to me when people call their parents by their first names," Braun said. "I know you two weren't close."

"It may have something to do with the fact she was more like a stranger to me," he reminded Braun. "I call most people by their first names. Calling her Iris seemed no different. I can see how somebody would think it's strange, but it really wasn't."

"How often did you see Wyatt, your stepfather?"

Braun went back to reading the print-outs that sat on the table next to him. He lifted one up and read it closely. He tried not to distract Jacob, but Braun couldn't ignore it. The document was a report of a missing person from 1991 out of a small town in Kentucky. *Victim: Weaver, Iris. Female, white, age thirty-eight. Reporting person: Wyatt Jones. Common-law husband.* Braun set the document aside to continue listening to Jacob. He kept the information to himself.

"All I knew was that Wyatt was with her the most. Out of all the men Iris had been with, this guy was the one that was around the most."

"Were they married? Do you know?"

"I don't know," Jacob stated. "Maybe I was the one that made it up in my mind. You know how a kid wants to believe something so bad you just begin to believe it. He treated me okay. I assumed they were married."

"Did he treat you like he was your stepfather?"

Jacob slouched backwards in his chair. "I don't even know what that means. I don't know what that feels like," he said. "Did he ever call me son? Hell no. I never thought that would happen anyway. He was just a man hanging around. Honestly, I waited for the day he was no longer in the picture."

"As you look back now, Jacob, why did you think he was your stepdad?"

"I'm sure I heard my grandma and aunt talking about him." He tried remembering. "My grandmother always asked Aunt Rose what she thought of the guy. Like, 'Rose, do you think they really got married?' Questions like that would come up. Aunt Rose would say she wasn't sure, but she would never put anything past Iris. You'd think they got married in Vegas or something. Does it really make a difference, Detective?"

"I'm just trying to understand Iris," Braun explained. "She was not very stable. And I'm not sure what role he played in that. What did you say his last name was?"

Braun wanted to compare the name to the one on the missing person report out of Kentucky.

"His name was Jones. Wyatt Jones."

"How long has it been since you've seen Wyatt Jones?"

"It's been a damn long time. I was very young."

"How young?"

"Since I was sixteen, I believe," he tried recalling.

"That seems odd to me."

Braun's laser-like focus on Wyatt had Jacob shook up. His face was suddenly pale. He began to sweat. Braun couldn't help but notice. He was worried Jacob was about to pass out. Jacob placed his head into his folded arms, on the table. Trying to calm his breathing. A panic attack?

"Iris goes missing just months earlier?" Braun reiterated. He watched Jacob's face.

Dead silence. Jacob stared straight forward. His breathing heavy now. He looked up.

"How do you explain seeing Wyatt months after your mother goes missing?" Braun questioned. "She didn't go back to Wyatt after she left the farm, did she? He didn't know where she was? Do you know if they were separated at the same time she went missing?"

An emptiness filled the seemingly shrinking interview room. Jacob stood up from his chair. He turned his back to Braun. His face still ashen. Beads of sweat on his upper forehead, just under his hairline. His right hand was shaking, so he stuffed it in his pocket. His balance was off-kilter. Braun stood and came around the table to make sure Jacob was not going to tumble over. His body language was shouting at Braun. He laid Jacob on the floor, until his blood pressure equalized. This was a turning point, but why? The extended focus on Wyatt was a shock to Jacob's central nervous system.

"I'm really nauseous," he said. "I could use some fresh air."

Detective Braun got Jacob to his feet, tested his balance, and guided him outside the interview room, down the hallway. They reached a door at the end. Braun opened it. A cool breeze hit them both in the face. It felt good to Braun. He realized how stuffy that small room really was. The sun was still bright. They were at the back of the building. No one around. Just a metal handrail leading down three concrete steps. It was as good a place as any for Jacob to sit and calm himself.

"Will you be okay out here?" Braun asked.

"I'll be fine," he said. "I'll feel better in a few minutes. Just let me sit here for a while. Alone, if that's okay? I won't take off on you, Braun."

"We've been talking too long," he said. "Take all the time you need out here."

Braun found an old brick on the ground just on the other side of the steps. He set it on the concrete, next to the door, propping it open. He pulled his handcuffs from their pouch, on his belt at the back of his pants.

"Don't take this the wrong way, Jacob, but I'm going to have to cuff you to the railing." It was not police procedure, but it would have to do.

"Don't trust me, huh?"

"I can't let my chief think I allowed you to sit out here by yourself," Braun explained. "You are still in my custody."

"I get it. If I walked away, that would be hard for you to explain."

"When you're ready to come back in, just holler down the hallway. I'll hear you. I'm going to work on getting you some food. I'm sure you're nauseous, because you haven't eaten for a while."

"That's not the reason, Detective," he admitted. "I'm just extremely nervous and it hit me all of a sudden. The talk about Wyatt spun me into a panic."

"You think you're having anxiety?"

"I've had anxiety as long as I remember," he said. "What I need to tell you has driven me into a panic attack."

"What do you need to tell me?"

"I've brought myself to this moment before," he said. "In my own mind. Just in my mind is all. I play this moment out over and over again, but I can't say the words I need to say out loud."

"I think I'm following," Braun said. "Now you are here. With me. It's no longer in your mind. This is the real-life situation you've imagined. You're ready to tell me something very important. It's good you are here, Jacob."

"There is nowhere to run any longer. There's nowhere to hide," he replied revealing the seriousness of his secret. "When I get my shit together out here, I need to come back and sit down. Man up. And tell you what really happened to Wyatt Jones."

"I'll leave you be for now," Braun said. "Get your bearings. The door is propped open. Shout for me. Let's get this done."

When Braun disappeared to the other side of the door, safely down the hallway, Jacob was able to finagle a half-smoked joint and book of matches from inside the elastic band at the top of his underwear, just under his jeans. Obviously missed when he was patted down. The joint was only an inch in length. He probably toked on it several times throughout the day, saving the stub for a quick fix. Jacob believed his stash of weed helped him deal with his anxiety. Tetrahydrocannabinol. THC. For Jacob, a wonder drug. That is at least what he told himself. He was able to light it, and then he took a long hard drag. Longer than usual. Held his breath for several seconds. Pulling the smoke deep into his lungs. Time was ticking. He needed to calm his nerves. Reduce his anxiety. Jacob finished the remainder of his joint and felt relaxed. Ready to talk. To roll the dice. Ready to move on and get this whole damn thing over with. Jacob shouted for Braun.

NINE

DETECTIVE BRAUN WAS BEGINNING to unravel some of Jacob's story. Was Jacob using the story of his grandfather to slowly open a more serious can of worms, in order to test Braun's reaction? It was as if he was slow-walking a story to test where it would get him regarding the three strikes law. Were there more serious crimes that occurred on that farm? Grandpa's death certainly wouldn't save Jacob from prison time. Jacob said that something played out in his mind. Something more dramatic.

Braun knew there was more. The past was grinding on Jacob's very soul. Torturing his brain. Eating at him minute by minute. It bogged down his life. Anxiety. Panic attacks. Frustration. Toxic memories were bombarding his existence. Relying on his weed to make it through the day? Something troubling him won't let him function for one day longer. Jacob seemed to be moving toward a revelation. Whichever direction this goes, wherever this leads, Braun needed to see this through and guide Jacob somewhere important. Braun wasn't sure exactly where, but it would be somewhere dark. Iris was missing for years? Where was Wyatt? Jacob didn't want to dive into these murky waters, where his dark past could destroy his future. Something of importance was about to be revealed.

Braun heard Jacob shout. He walked down the hallway, as he scanned a new print-out just received from the Kentucky Department of Corrections. As he suspected, Wyatt Alan Jones had spent roughly three hundred sixty-five days in jail for a drug charge, cocaine to be exact, around the same time Iris went missing. Braun unfastened the handcuffs from the railing. He could smell the burnt cannabis on Jacob's body. He ignored the odor. Jacob looked at Braun. Shrugged. An empty matchbook sat in the gravel five feet from Jacob. No sign of the joint. Braun said nothing. It wasn't worth knowing how he got his hands on it.

"I got you a bottle of pop. It's on the table," Braun said. "I wasn't sure if you needed anything to drink. I'm having some food brought up as well. A sandwich and chips."

"Thanks." Jacob was calmer. Seemed to be more relaxed. Hungry, too.

He sat back down at the interview room table. Braun noticed the difference in his demeanor. More upright. Straight-forward in his gaze, although a little hazy. Jacob's grip on something had loosened, the palpable tension had slackened. Was he finally opening up? Giving in?

"Do you feel like talking now, about whatever is eating at you, Jacob?"

"I do," he said. "Do you feel like listening? You must be as tired as I am."

"I sensed a feeling of urgency before you went and got some fresh air."

"Things come over me," he admitted. "It's hard to explain. I'm never quite sure when it's going to happen. But the past somehow falls over me like a dark cloud. Out of nowhere. Years ago, can seem like yesterday. Guilt hits me hard. Bam. Just like that."

"About Wyatt Jones?"

"Yeah, good old Wyatt," he said, slowly leaning forward. His eyes revealed a searching for the right words. "Wyatt was different."

Braun sat silent. He didn't want to interrupt Jacob's thought process. He had a feeling he was about to reveal something important.

"He came around the farm, off and on. There was no rhyme or reason," he explained. "Sometimes he came with Iris, and sometimes she came alone. Like a hanger-on. The guy had nothing to do. Didn't ever work. Whenever he came, he was quiet. Always seemed to be in the background. He sat and watched everyone else. Was probably there just to get whatever it was that Iris came to get."

"And what was it that they wanted to get, Jacob?"

"Money. Usually money," he smirked. "To feed the beast, I suppose."

"How did they get there?"

"What do you mean?"

"How did they get around? Car? Bus?"

"An old car."

"Was it Wyatt's?"

"No way," he said. "Iris' car. She drove it, but it was an old Buick Grandpa let her drive. It was in his name though. She never really owned it."

"So, your grandpa's car," Braun confirmed, and made a note.

"She couldn't afford her own. Spent any extra money on dope. She'd come to the farm whenever she needed something. She knew Grandpa would check it over. Change the oil if needed. Kick the tires."

"I thought there was animosity between the two of them."

"There was plenty of hostility," he answered, "but, the car was Grandpa's. He did it for himself and not for her. He planned on getting that car back someday. He had no intention of giving it to her. She had a way of slowly taking things, over time."

"When did all of that change?"

"It all changed the day she took off," he said. "She left the car behind, probably after one of their arguments. Maybe he put his foot down and told her she couldn't have the car anymore. I can't say, because I wasn't there."

"So, you didn't witness what prompted her leaving that day?"

"No, but I witnessed the fact that she was gone and the car was still at the farm," he said, "parked right by the shed where she always parked it."

"And Wyatt?"

"Wyatt wasn't with her," he clarified. "She was alone. You never knew when he was going to be with her. The man was unreliable. Perfect fit for Iris."

"When did you see Wyatt again?"

"It had to be about six months later."

"Why do you remember that?"

"Because he came alone," he said. "That wouldn't seem odd for anyone else, but it was unusual for Wyatt. Iris alone was not strange, but Wyatt wouldn't come there alone. No way. There weren't many reasons for him to come to the farm without her. There had to be something wrong."

"So, if the car was left behind by Iris," he probed, "then, how did Wyatt get to the farm?"

"He drove his motorcycle," he explained. "That was all he talked about. His old Harley. But I had never seen it, because they always drove up in Iris' car. Grandpa's Buick. Wyatt was from the Paducah, Kentucky area. He was not going to drive an old Harley too far with Iris on the back."

"Understood," Braun said. "So, why did Wyatt come this time, alone? You thought that was strange behavior on his part, right?"

"I did. And it turned into a real fucking mess," he said. "A mess I can't shake from my mind."

"What happened?"

"Wyatt appeared out of nowhere, in the early evening. I remember that," he said, "because I had just gotten home and the sun was low. I would say it was six or seven o'clock."

"Who was all there?"

"Who was always there? Grandpa, Grandma and Aunt Rose. And me, of course."

"What happened?"

"We heard the motorcycle. Which was odd, like I said, because we hadn't heard a motorcycle ever pull up the driveway at the farmhouse? Grandpa is like, 'What in the hell is that racket?' I said 'it sounds like a motorcycle.' Aunt Rose got up off her chair and looked out the window. 'It's Wyatt,' she said quietly in a subdued, questioning tone. Like she was trying to figure out why. He came to the door and Aunt Rose let him in," he explained. "And he was really pissed off from the very git-go, which didn't sit well with Grandma. Came in the door all huffing and puffing mad. That was a Wyatt I'd never seen."

"Angry about what?"

"Started yelling right away, 'Where in the hell is Iris? I haven't seen that woman in months. Where did she take off to this time? I know you told her to stay away from me, didn't you?'"

"'Slow down there, Wyatt!' Grandpa yelled. Grandma told him that if he wanted to talk about Iris he was going to have to simmer down."

"Did he?"

"He quieted down, at least his voice, but I could still see that he was angry as hell."

"How was all this sitting with Aunt Rose?"

"She was calm. She knew Wyatt and how he could be," he remembered. "I always thought Aunt Rose had Wyatt figured out. She was never upset with him. Always understood him. The guy was usually pretty laid back. Except for that night. He was really pissed."

"What was different about that night?" he asked. "Other than Wyatt questioning Iris' whereabouts? He knew she disappeared now and then."

"I figured he was the one that always knew where she was. She only disappeared from the farm. From us, the family. My family. Never him. He was her only constant."

"What did he want? What were you suppose to do?"

"Wyatt was suspicious."

"Of who? Of what?"

"He was using words, like foul play. Like he was accusing us of something."

"Was he blaming one of you for Iris going missing?"

"Not at first. He was testing everybody," he explained. "As the evening went, he pushed harder. You know, he became more and more accusatory."

"How so?"

"He began to get into it with my aunt. Questioning the tense relationship between her and Iris," he said. "He was really pushing my aunt Rose hard."

"Wyatt thought that led to violence?" Braun probed. "It's a stretch to get to foul play. Did things get worse that night?"

"Much worse."

"Wyatt was threatening?"

"My aunt Rose told Wyatt that if he was going to accuse the family of something so crazy, it was time for him to leave."

"But it was late at night by now, right?" Braun asked, trying to nail down a timeframe in the story unfolding before him. He anticipated being told something bad had happened, but what? "What did Wyatt do, or say?"

"'I need a cigarette. I'm going outside.'"

"You need a cigarette?"

"No, no...not me," he said. "That is exactly what Wyatt said after my aunt told him he should leave. He said, 'I need a cigarette. I'm going outside.' I knew that he wanted to start snooping around. Smoking was just an excuse."

"Where did he want to snoop?"

"The farm, I assumed," he said. "I felt as though he wanted to look around at the barn, the shed and silo. Start snooping anywhere."

"What did he do next?"

"I watched him go outside. I walked over to the front porch and sat in the rocking chair and just watched him. I saw him light up a cigarette and approach the car that Iris drove. Grandpa's Buick. It was parked by the shed. He walked around it, looking inside all the windows. Popped the trunk and looked in. I don't know what he thought he was going to find. Did he think she was lying in the car? In the trunk?"

Braun let Jacob talk. He was in the flow.

"He walked into the shed. I saw the light bulb come on. The shed is very small. It didn't take him long to look inside," he explained. "There's no way she could've been in there. I saw the light go off."

"What time of night was it now, Jacob?"

"It had to be somewhere around eight or so. Maybe eight-thirty," he guessed. "I can't really remember, but it was getting dark out. I remember the darkness for sure. A black sky. Clouds blocked the stars, so not much outside light."

"Did Wyatt keep searching?"

"He walked away from the shed, but it was so damn dark I lost complete sight of him," he recalled. "Then, I saw the sudden orange glow off the tip of his cigarette. He must have taken a good hard drag. He was heading toward the barn."

"How far was the barn from where you were sitting on the porch?"

"I'd say a hundred feet. Maybe, hundred-fifty."

"Could you see him anymore or just the glow off his cigarette?"

"Just the glow. I got up off the chair and walked down off the porch," he described. "As I walked toward the barn I could see the faint outline of his body walking around the barn. I got closer and watched him. Where was he going? That's what I was wondering."

"Why were you worried about what he was doing?" Braun asked. "Why not let him take a look around the farm and be done with it?"

"Because he was so angry. He was accusatory. He all but accused us of doing something bad to Iris," he said. "Does that sound like a guy that could be trusted alone?"

"What did you think he might do?"

"I wasn't thinking straight at the time," he admitted. "Was he going to take that cigarette and start the barn on fire? Wyatt was different. I told you how he was. Now, he was really pissed off. He seemed unhinged."

"Did you ever catch up to him?"

"I did."

"Still by the barn?"

"He was now at the back of the barn," he described. "I walked up to him and asked him if he had found what he was looking for. He thought I was being a smartass. Actually, I was serious."

"Was he angry at you now?"

"He told me that Iris had never skipped out on him for more than a few days at a time," he stated. "A week at most. He said that there was no way possible that Iris would ever leave him for that long. He was convinced something bad had happened to her."

"Now you must have known what he was accusing your family of."

"I told him that Iris had left the farm and our family for a lot more than six months at a time," he explained. "I told him that six months wasn't something I had ever considered worth getting shook up about. I told him I never knew from one month to the next if she would ever come back."

"That pissed him off?" Braun assumed.

"He told me that Iris didn't have to answer to me. That I was just a teenager," he said. "Then, he threw his cigarette down in the mud right between my feet."

"Your honest opinions of her set him off."

"I did tell him that no mother should ever abandon her kid," he recalled. "I told Wyatt she was worthless. I said she was a failure. I told him she was a failure as a person, not just a mother. I was pissed now. Who is he to act like she was good?"

"What did Wyatt do?"

"He looked at me and didn't say a fricking word."

"He didn't do anything?"

"I never said that…I just said that he never said a word," Jacob reacted. "He stood there for about five seconds and looked me straight in the eyes. Quiet and all. It was so dark. It was as if our eyes were the only source of light. All of a sudden, he stepped into me. Close. I could smell the cigarette on his breath. He was so close he put his right hand on my shoulder. Our noses almost touched. I tried to step back, but he held me there. I thought for a moment he wanted to tell me something.

Like there was something he wanted to whisper. Then, it was like he decided that whatever he had to say should be kept to himself."

"You were scared he was going to hurt you?"

"He pushed me off to the side and walked past me. Toward the silo," he said. "There's a small pen next to the silo, where we used to keep some pigs, and goats. Animals like that. I saw him tilt his head to the side and light another cigarette. He leaned against a fence post and just stared up into the dark sky. Smoking. Like he was thinking of what to do next. He looked down into that muddy pen. It was no more than thirty by thirty feet. The fence was old, and beat up. Worn out. Partially broken down. He just stared into that pen."

"What did you do?"

"I walked over to where he was standing. Where he was looking."

Braun continued to scratch down notes. He slid his chair up closer to the table, bumping the edge and spilling some of Jacob's pop on the table. Jacob ignored the mess. He stood and turned his back on Braun. Important body language for sure. Uncertain. Silent. Afraid?

"He kept staring. Gazing, in a trance, into that pen," he explained. "And then he turned toward me, without warning. I thought maybe I had startled him."

Jacob turned back around, facing Braun again. "Wyatt could feel me right up on him."

"Was there any lighting in the area?"

"Just one light at the peak of the barn, right next to the silo," he recalled. "It didn't give off much light. It just put a faint haze over the pen."

"Like a fog?"

"Yeah, like a fog."

"Could you still see Wyatt?"

"I could see him," he whispered. "As he turned around, to face me, the light bounced off the blade he was holding in his hand."

"A knife?"

"In his right hand," he said. "His cigarette was in his left."

Braun leaned forward, physically pressing Jacob for more, waiting for a revelation he knew was coming.

"He told me, 'What if I killed you, right now, like someone killed Iris?'"

"I told him he was fucking crazy," he said. "Nobody killed Iris! She took off just like she always did. Why would he think anyone killed her?"

"Did he threaten you with the knife?"

"This was where things really went bad," he continued. "Wyatt started getting loud again. He started screaming at me, telling me that something bad had happened to Iris and somebody in this family knew about it. He raised the knife up toward my chin. I froze for a minute and just listened. I thought he was going to cut my throat. I had never seen Wyatt this crazy. He was yelling shit, like this farm was fucking cursed. Grandpa's farm was evil. He said that the farm held secrets that even I knew nothing about. It was some very heavy shit. Especially for Wyatt. He was never the kind of man that opened up and shouted stupid stuff like that. That was not the Wyatt I knew."

"What did he do with the knife?"

"He placed the blade sideways, against my neck," he alleged. "Yelling, 'Where is she, Jacob?'"

Notes were being written fast and furious. Braun looked down at his recorder. He saw the cassette reels whirling. *This is being recorded,* he thought to himself...relieved.

"I thought I was dead," he admitted. "I thought he might kill me."

Braun kept silent and looked up, into Jacob's eyes.

"I reached up and grabbed the blade as tightly as I could." He stood and illustrated.

Jacob opened the palm of his hand and showed Detective Braun a four-to-five-inch permanent scar.

"I pulled the blade downward, trying to keep it away from my neck. He pulled the blade from my hand, causing this slice here, but I grabbed the handle with my other hand and we struggled. I was in a rage by now. I felt a sense of strength come over me. Survival mode had kicked in. I had never experienced such a rush of adrenaline."

The pen Braun was using unexpectedly ran out of ink. He noticed the last few words of his notes had gradually faded. He threw the pen in the garbage can that sat in the corner of the room, by the door. He reflexively grasped the second pen by the side of his notepad and retraced the words that had seemed to disappear from the page. He looked up at Jacob.

"I think Wyatt was convinced in his mind that, somehow, I was behind the disappearance of Iris. He totally lost it," he alleged. "I despised her, Detective. I'll admit that. I hated who she became. But it was because of what she did, not so much for who she was. I know that sounds weird, but I always believed she could be a good person, if she just tried. It was the things she did I hated. The drugs and drinking. I never once thought of harming her. She left me. Left us. Left the farm. I never harmed her."

"How did this all end with Wyatt?"

"We struggled. Struggled hard. I didn't know what it was to fight for my life. We fell to the muddy ground just outside the pen," he described. "We wrestled on the ground until we were pinned against the base of the silo. That is when he quit. He just stopped fighting. It was like he was moving in slow motion or something. He tried to stand. He could barely get up to his feet. I just stepped back and gave him space. I didn't know what was going on."

"He was injured?"

"I knew something was terribly wrong," he admitted. "Wyatt turned slightly to the side. He leaned up against the silo. You know, with one hand. It was as if nothing had just happened between us. I think I remember him lighting up another cigarette. It was strange. As he turned away from the silo, the dim light from the barn exposed half his body. I saw the handle of the knife sticking out of his left side. Just the handle. From underneath his ribs. The blade was deep inside him. I didn't want it to happen. It was all so surreal. I hoped he would be able to pull the knife out. Can you pull a knife out like that?"

Braun pressed for more.

"He started laughing at me, Braun."

"Laughing?"

"It was eerie. He was so loud, and it sounded devious," he said. "He was yelling, 'Do ya see what I mean about this fucking farm, Jacob? See what in the hell I mean? She's here. Iris is here. Nearby. Rose knows exactly where she is.'"

"What did he do with the knife?" Braun probed. "He was still talking? Weren't you afraid he was seriously wounded? Were you afraid he'd die?"

"It didn't make any difference what I thought at that moment," he grimaced. "It just didn't make a bit of difference. What could I do? I had no control over what happened next."

"I don't get what you mean, Jacob. Why didn't it make a difference?"

"I need a goddamn break, Braun." Jacob shoved himself back further into his chair. He pulled both legs, and his heels, up onto the chair and wrapped his arms around his knees. Like a child, in a semi-fetal position, frightened of what came next. "I think I'm going to puke."

"Let's get you to the bathroom," Braun said, as he quickly stood. He opened the door, and let him out.

TEN

JACOB MADE HIS WAY down the hallway to the bathroom. There were trickles of puke on the tile floor, like liquid bread crumbs for Braun to track. He heard Jacob vomiting in the stall. The echo rang down the hallway. Jacob, somewhat shaky, returned. Weak. Pale. The blood had drained from his entire face and neck. A morbid expression took its place. Making Jacob look instantly emaciated.

As Braun approached the truth, Jacob was weakening. Perhaps, his anxiety. Angst. Releasing the words was revealing the pain held so deep. Words he could not completely release from his lips at one time in his life, now formed the truth. But, who's truth? What held him back at this point? Braun could see that Jacob was already describing a traumatic experience. One he had lived with for years. The darkness, the violence, the blood.

Braun's mind suddenly took him back to Vietnam. It was one of the first times in years he had not been able to drive the memories back into their hiding place. His first kill was as vivid now as it was then. He was taking point for his recon team, on the border of Laos, near Phu Bai, when he was attacked by a lone Viet Cong soldier that had fallen behind his unit. Braun saw the bright flash of his enemy's knife swipe at his body. They struggled on the slimy green plants of the jungle, Braun trying to avoid getting slashed. He knew a severe laceration could cause him to bleed out, which meant losing strength.

Braun had very little sleep, as did every soldier. Two hours a night was not uncommon. It was adrenaline that kept him awake, in the fight for his life. Braun was on his back, his left hand holding the wrist of his combatant. He was able to get his right hand on the handle of his KA-BAR and pull it from its sheath. As his rival jerked his wrist free from Braun's grip, Braun swung his knife hard and fast, burying the blade deep into his side. He knew the sharp steel had penetrated a vital organ, the kidney or spleen. Perhaps, a lung. The sensation of the blade penetrating human flesh was unlike anything Braun had ever experienced. A loud gasp of air released from the VC soldier's lung, like the swoosh of a shriveling balloon. Death was imminent. For Braun, there would be more killing over the next two years of his hell on earth.

WHAT ABOUT JACOB'S description of Wyatt's behavior? Was he on drugs? Or overwhelmed with paranoia? What did he know? What had Iris told Wyatt when they were alone, far away from the hold the farm seemed to have on everyone? And even if Wyatt was wrong to blame the Weavers, one question lingered. Where in the hell was Iris?

They were hours into the interview. Jacob appeared determined to reveal whatever it was that haunted him. After his brutal fight with Wyatt, what was it that didn't make any difference? Jacob had whispered, *it didn't make any difference.*

Braun continued his questioning.

"Are you okay to keep going?"

Jacob paced as he ran both hands through his hair and sighed heavily. Braun was standing at the door, waiting, wondering if they would continue.

"Let me sit for a minute," he said. "I want to talk. I need to get this out."

"It's time, Jacob."

"Where was I?" he asked, rubbing his face, and moving his head side to side, up and down, expanding his eyes wide, forcing himself into readiness.

"Wyatt was on his feet, the knife was sticking out of his side," Braun prompted.

"Yes," he continued. "That is when it happened."

"What happened?"

"Someone came around from the backside of the silo," he recalled.

"You couldn't see who it was?"

"Not at first. It was still very dark. That light on the barn was dim," he said. "All of a sudden, a shovel struck Wyatt in the back of the head. He didn't know what hit him. He went down hard. Really hard. I mean, I heard his skull crack. The knife was still in his side. It was pitch black out, like I said. The lighting was terrible."

"Who struck Wyatt?"

"Aunt Rose. She stepped into the light," he depicted. "She was still holding the shovel tightly in both hands. It must have been leaning against the silo. I never saw it, because it was around the backside. Wyatt was not moving. At all. There was complete silence. No more talking. No more fighting. My hand was cut and still bleeding. Aunt Rose told me what to do. Like she always did. 'I'll clean up the mess.' That's what she told me."

"What did she tell you to do?"

"She saw that I was in a daze. It was all the adrenaline. All the blood," he explained. "She knew I was in shock. I wasn't thinking straight. It was like a bad dream. I had tunnel vision. Everything went into slow motion."

"What did you do with Wyatt?" Braun pushed. "Did you help him? Was he alive?"

"I assumed he was dead," he admitted. "He wasn't moving. I mean, he was very still. The kind of stillness that is beyond someone just passed out or sleeping. It was stillness beyond still. It's hard to describe, but it was a stillness that makes you know. We both knew. Aunt Rose knew."

"What did you do with Wyatt?" he demanded.

"I didn't do anything," he said. "Aunt Rose grabbed me by the shoulders and pulled her face into mine. So she could really see into my eyes. 'Go to Ronnie's place. Right now, Jacob. Get to Ronnie's place.'"

"Ronnie?"

"Yeah."

"You went to his house?"

"Rode my bike there. It was late. Dark. There are no lights on Old Johnson Road."

"What did Aunt Rose do?"

"She yelled at me as I rode away, 'Jacob, I will take care of all this. Don't worry. Remember, Wyatt was trying to stab you. He could have killed you.' She told me to get going and to spend the night at Ronnie's. To tell Ronnie I needed a place to stay for one night. Not to tell him about what happened. Tell him I got mad and cut my hand on a broken window. That I got in an argument with Grandpa, or something like that. Anything. He'd believe me. Aunt Rose was right. Ronnie would believe anything I told him."

"Did Rose tell you what she did with Wyatt?"

"We never spoke about it, so I can only assume what she did."

"She got rid of Wyatt's body?"

"She cleaned up the mess. Fixed the problem."

"Jacob. Do you hear yourself? You make it sound like somebody just spilled a bowl of soup on the floor," Braun lectured. "What does clean up the mess really mean? We are talking about a human being, Jacob. What did she do with Wyatt?"

"She got rid of him," he revealed. "His body . . . his clothes."

"His motorcycle?" Braun questioned. "A motorcycle is no small thing to get rid of."

"I don't know for sure, but I do know that by noon the next day I was back on the farm and there was no sign of Wyatt. There was no sign of his motorcycle. They were gone."

"Who killed Wyatt?" he demanded a straight answer.

"I did. I think. Yes, I must have. I feel like I was the one responsible. Because of the fight. I'm not one to put the blame on someone else. I stabbed him. I suppose Aunt Rose would say she did," he speculated. "We both did? How do I know for sure?"

"You're saying it was self-defense?"

"Does it make a fucking difference what I say?" he shouted. "Isn't that up to someone else to decide? Someone like you, Braun? Or people on a jury. Or a judge. I'm just trying to tell you what I thought happened that night. What I recall. It's a blur now after all these years."

"What did your grandma and grandpa know?"

"They thought Wyatt got pissed off and left," he replied, "and went back to Kentucky."

"Did you ever talk about the fight?"

"Not with them, specifically, no," he recalled, "but why would I bring it up to them?"

"You are telling me there was complete silence in the house about Wyatt? After all the arguing?"

"Yes. Dead silence. That is all there was. That's all there ever was."

"To me, the silence from Grandma and Grandpa meant they knew exactly what happened," Braun concluded. "Otherwise, wouldn't they be asking questions? What happened to Wyatt? Where is he? Where's his motorcycle?"

"That may seem logical," he said, "but, in our family, their silence meant for me to be silent and let whatever happened go. Just let it all go."

"I see. That was how Aunt Rose wanted it?"

"I was told to go to Ronnie's. And I went."

"The fact of the matter is Wyatt is buried somewhere on your grandpa's property," he theorized. "You'd agree with that?"

"I can't imagine Aunt Rose hauling his body and a motorcycle away in the middle of the night," he agreed. "Where would she go? Where would she take him? A fricking motorcycle, for God's sake."

"Jacob, this question is important. Has anyone else ever lived on the Weaver farm, since your grandmother passed away?" he asked. "Renters? Farmhands? And I mean someone other than Aunt Rose?"

"If you don't count me, Aunt Rose is the only one."

"And in the last fourteen years, has she ever spoken about Wyatt?"

"Never even whispered his name," Jacob confirmed. "It was as if Wyatt never existed."

"Maybe the only way to live with murder is to pretend it never happened," Braun said. "Maybe she felt Wyatt deserved to die. Maybe she wanted Wyatt dead for other reasons."

Jacob sat stone-faced. The muscles in his body went limp. A certain weight had been lifted. He leaned his elbows onto the table in front of him and placed both hands over his face. A heavy sigh. Silence revealed a sign of relief. Jacob realized that he had found a way to live with the haunting memory of Wyatt's murder all these years. At that very moment, Frank Braun realized he had been doing the exact same thing.

ELEVEN

DETECTIVE BRAUN HAD a crime scene to secure. The entire Weaver farm. He needed to get to Aunt Rose. Where is Wyatt's body? Where is the motorcycle? Where is Iris? Aunt Rose had to know Jacob was in jail. She was a smart woman. She knew everything about Jacob. Where he is at any moment. Where he goes when he leaves the farm. Rose knew Jacob was being questioned. She also knew that her tightly woven nest was about to unravel. Was she at the farm preparing for the collapse of her secret world?

Detective Braun put the next steps into motion. And the next one was to find out what Rose knew. The last chapter of Jacob's story may be one of deep regret and misery. Aunt Rose held the key to the rest of this dysfunctional saga. Perhaps, more than anyone, it was Rose that knew the true secrets hidden somewhere on that farm. Was Jacob an unwitting player? Grandma and Grandpa were gone. Wyatt gone. Iris gone? Jacob treading water. Slipping under, drowning in panic, gagging for air, gasping for the breath that keeps him alive long enough to reveal the entire truth. Was he ready to abandon his own freedom? After all, he just confessed to killing a man. Braun knew that those dark secrets slowly rust the heart. Kill the life-spirit. They could make a grown man crumble, like a weather-worn silo.

Braun called Prosecutor Thomas. She needed to know that things were moving quickly. She also needed to know that Jacob had opened up about a serious crime and that Braun was on his way to the Weaver family farm to secure the evidence. Thomas would stress that word, more than any other. Evidence. Evidence. Evidence. A good prosecutor's mantra. Without evidence all she had was a story and stories could be fabricated. A false story would give Jacob something to think about as he sits in prison. Braun knew Grandpa Weaver's death was one of those ambiguous stories. True or not, it was not going to move the needle, when it came to Prosecutor Thomas. He rang her on the phone.

"Thomas."

"It's Braun."

"You must be onto something," she assumed. "You know the arraignment is still in the morning, right? I'm going forward on the felony drug charges."

"I knew you would. I'm going to the farm now."

"You must have some evidence?" she asked. "Am I to assume this isn't about Grandpa anymore? Grandpa's story won't save this guy's ass you know."

"A guy named Jones."

"Say again."

"Wyatt Jones," Braun repeated. "A missing person out of Kentucky."

"What do you have on him?"

"He's buried on that farm."

"No shit. Keep me posted," she demanded. "I'll trade a dead body for a box of weed any day of the week. Solve it, Braun."

"Will do. I'm not quite there yet," Braun admitted. "There is somebody at the farm I need to confront."

Braun opened the interview room door. He leaned over and placed both hands flat on the table top. "Jacob. It is time to go."

"Go?"

"To the farm," he said. "We need to get to the farm."

"Why am I going?"

"I need you there," Braun said. "You have revealed your life to me. Your honesty has brought us to this point."

"Will I have to face Aunt Rose?" he worried. "I already know she's angry with me."

"How do you know that?"

"She was the one call I made after I got arrested."

"So, she's known this whole time you've been here?" he indicated. "With me?"

"I told her about your article, and how I was going to try and talk to you."

"What did she say?"

"Keep my mouth shut. Not to say a word about anything," he acknowledged. "She told me that after all these years, it would be the biggest mistake I could ever make."

"What did you tell her?" Braun asked. "Did she threaten you?"

"She didn't really threaten me," he explained, "but, she told me that I would be changing both of our lives forever."

"You broke free from her grasp, Jacob. You ignored her," Braun stated. "This was a first for you, wasn't it?"

"Yes," he confessed, "but, for some reason, I didn't think I would ever have to face her again."

"I won't make you face her unless you want to," Braun promised. "I just need you nearby. Just in case I need you for persuasion. Or confirmation of things she tells me. That is if she talks to me at all. As far as I'm concerned you can stay in my car until I need you."

"I've got to face Aunt Rose someday," he realized.

"It's time to go then."

BOTH MEN GOT INTO Braun's unmarked vehicle and made their way to the farm. Seven miles down Old Johnson Road. The trip was eerily quiet. Neither man spoke. Jacob stared out the window. Watched as the telephone poles flew by like rigid toothpicks. One by one. Counting them like a bored child. This trip to the farm was different. As if the farm waited for him. To challenge him to further seek the truth. To find the answers to the mysteries of Jacob's life. Mysteries even he was not aware of.

Braun drove deliberately up the long and winding driveway. Lined with tall evergreens. One burnt orange from death. The old gravel path had been taken over years ago by quack grass and yellow nutsedge, the crushed limestone barely visible. Braun was struck with a strong feeling of déjà vu. The farmhouse was two stories, faded whitewash board, on a stone block foundation, full wraparound porch, floorboards missing, and one end drooping from rot. The collapsing work shed was surrounded by buckhorn plantain and thick patches of chickweed. An old clothesline still stood, but sagged low, touching the ground in the middle. Braun noticed a wooden porch swing, painted in John Deere green, hanging from porch beams at the front of the house. The swing faced a long narrow yard, surrounded on both sides by massive willow trees, their branches drooping to the ground. Rusted chains. Eye bolts slackened and giving way. The faded green paint chipped and curled. Braun suddenly recalled that very swing. It seemed pleasant and relaxing seventeen years earlier. The Weaver family farm now came back to him in full. Rosemary Weaver was the woman he remembered. The woman that took custody of Jacob that day. All those years seemed like a lifetime ago.

Aunt Rose had let all the little things deteriorate. Those were the daily chores that Grandpa addressed. Rose focused on tending to her garden. Her garden of secrets. Tending to the pain and regret that lingered with a pungent odor of rot in the country air. Braun noticed the aging weathered barn. A familiar white color, faded over time, the hint of metal gray seeping out from deep within. Pockmarked from the punishing sun and relentless spring rains. Human neglect.

Right next to the barn was an abandoned silo. At least twenty feet high, with old concrete stave panels strengthened by steel bands at the staves' edges. A time-stamp of the not-too-distant past. An iron ladder was attached to the backside. For a young child, seeking the mysteries on a quiet farm, the rungs reached toward the sky and the bright stars on a black fall night. Jacob had climbed those steel rungs hundreds of times. To think. To read. To watch. To wonder what lay beyond the fields of corn and beans. Take your troubles to the silo, Aunt Rose would tell him. So, he would climb to the top. Gaze over the furrowed land. Tell himself all would be okay. He looked at those structures once again, as if it was the first time he had truly seen them. He also watched Frank Braun. A man he had come to trust. The man he had drawn profoundly into his personal woe.

"Stay in the car, Jacob," Braun ordered. "I'm going to check the house for Aunt Rose."

"If she's not there, I might know where she is," he whispered.

"I'll be back."

"Braun..."

"Yes..."

"Don't hurt her," he said.

"There's no reason to hurt anyone," Braun reassured. "I just need to talk to her."

Detective Braun walked to the porch. The screen door was limp and open. One hinge hung loose. No lock. He pushed it open and called out for Rose. No response. He stepped further inside until he reached another door. Made of heavy oak, with a brass knob, open two inches. He slowly swung it wide open. Called out for Rose again. Again, no response. Due to the circumstances, a welfare check of Rose was legal and necessary. He walked in further calling her name. Over and over. Was she hurt? No one was in the house. There were signs. Life was obvious. Food in the kitchen. Newspapers stacked by a lounge chair. Knitting equipment sitting on top of a stack of magazines. Braun recalled his own mother. *Knit one, purl two.* The house was empty. He walked back out to his car. Jacob was trying to speak through the car window.

"The silo," Jacob mumbled. He pointed.

Braun leaned down by the window. "Say again."

"Check the silo."

Braun looked east and saw the old barn and neglected silo standing there. A certain loneliness. Reminders of better days gone by. He walked toward the silo. Why the silo? Jacob had his reasons. He suspected things Braun would find out on his own. He continued to walk until he reached the bottom of the silo. He saw the small muddy pen that Jacob had described during his fight with Wyatt.

"I knew you'd come!" she shouted. Frank looked behind him. All around. *Where is she?*

Rose's voice was muffled. It was from another place. Braun looked up, blocking the sun's glare, toward the sky. Toward her voice. Aunt Rose was sitting atop the silo. Alone. The sun still burned, but was beginning to lower in the west. It was peaceful and beautiful. Rose watched intently. Looking down at Detective Braun and then looking outward again, across the vast fields of the Weaver land. She looked like a woman who was resigned to a fate she had resisted for years. For just a moment, her look of resignation was like the one Braun noticed on Jacob's face as he finally opened up about Wyatt's murder.

"Are you okay up there?"

"Is Jacob with you?"

"He stayed back in the car, Rose."

"I would rather have him here. Near me," she said. "There are things I need him to hear."

"I'll try to get him over here."

Braun looked back at his car. He saw Jacob roll down the window and stick his head out. Braun waved him over to the silo. He knew what Braun wanted. He got out of the car and timidly ambled, hesitantly, toward them both. Anxious. Defensive. Afraid of the ending to his turmoil. Afraid of what he anticipated. Jacob reached the silo and looked upward. He sadly remembered her words as he grew up. *Take your troubles to the silo.*

"I'm sorry, Jacob," she bellowed. "I'm sorry you have to see me like this."

"Don't say that, Aunt Rose," he said. "I don't blame you."

"You should," she replied. "I deserve blame. I am not who you think I am."

"Stop it. Please. Stop talking like that."

"There are things you don't know," she said. "Now is the time to tell Detective Braun everything."

"I've told him everything already."

"Are you going to climb down from there, Rose?" Braun asked, "so we can talk to each other face to face. We can go into your house and sit at the table."

"You'll hear everything I have to say from right here, Detective," she responded. "If you try to come up here and get me, you will make the situation much worse. If you want to hear what I have to say, stay right where you are."

"I can speak with you anywhere," he said. "I just want to make sure you're comfortable while we talk."

Braun knew this was far from an ideal setup for talking to Rose. She was in complete control of the immediate environment, both physically and psychologically. She loomed large above Braun. He knew the power balance was now off. Making him feel small. He was not in control of the situation. He wasn't surprised, though, because Jacob described Rose as a woman that controlled everyone in her circle of influence. Now Braun was in that circle.

"No sense in being comfortable," she quipped. "I have never lived one moment, in all my years, feeling comfortable. Why worry about it now?"

"Come down from there, Aunt Rose," Jacob begged. "There's no reason for you to be up there. I've told Detective Braun all he needs to know. We can move on now."

"You've told him lies, Jacob," she demanded, "and you didn't even know it."

"That's crazy," he replied. "I told him the truth."

Braun took two measured steps forward, while Jacob was occupying Rose. He grabbed the third steel rung up on the ladder, testing its sturdiness. Rose noticed his attempt.

"Don't try it, Detective. I'm deadly serious. Do not try climbing that ladder."

"Come down," Jacob repeated. "I can't talk to you while you're up there."

"You told the detective a story, Jacob. Your story. You've shared one truth. Yours. But you didn't tell the whole truth. Because, you don't know the whole truth."

"I told Braun about Wyatt. He knows what happened," he assured her. "What else is there worth talking about?"

"The whole story," she said. "Things happened before you were even born, which has led up to this very moment. You can stand there and listen, or you can leave, Jacob. Whichever you choose, it is time to tell Detective Braun what he wants to know."

Jacob tried to grab the rungs on the ladder of the silo. Braun had an awful sensation. One of apprehension. Dread. He grabbed Jacob by the arm and stopped him from moving further.

Jacob backed off. Resignation followed. Once again, Jacob found himself submitting to Aunt Rose's wishes. The kind of compliance he lived with all his life. Jacob was noticeably dejected. Vulnerable, due to his lack of control. He physically collapsed to the ground. Chickweed surrounding him, like camouflage for a helpless fawn. He could only wait.

"I'm done, Aunt Rose," he accepted.

"When I'm finished, Jacob," she answered. "You will finally be free. You'll have a long life ahead of you, without the shackles of this farm and the dark memories that grew like those weeds around you."

"Where do we begin, Rose?" Braun asked. He continued to stand and look up to the top of the silo as she sat on the rim's rusted edge.

"I need to start with Jacob," she said. "He is all I ever cared about."

Jacob was now sitting on the ground. Braun found an old rusty red metal water trough, pulled it up next to Jacob and sat on the rim.

"It was three days before you were born," she said. "Iris showed up to the farm. She had Wyatt in tow. She had nowhere else to go. And under the circumstances it was best she came to the farm. The whole thing was a damn mess. She said she had been sick. She didn't look well. I knew it was the drugs and the alcohol. But Iris was more than sick. She was pregnant. With you. It's hard to believe, but she never knew she was pregnant. Iris was already about to give birth. I could hardly tell she was pregnant. She had no weight gain. So thin and weak."

"Why didn't you take her to the hospital?" Jacob questioned.

"That isn't what you do as a Weaver," she harshly responded. "Her water broke and I knew. In her condition, she refused to go anyway. There was no time to leave the farm. Not in her condition. When I told her she was giving birth, she was in denial. She told me she wasn't even pregnant. That was the drugs talking. I knew whatever was going to happen to her was going to happen."

"Where was Wyatt?" Braun probed.

"Right where I told him to be," she replied. "Out of the room and downstairs, where he wouldn't get in the way. When baby girl Weaver was delivered, Iris was hysterical."

"Baby girl Weaver?" Jacob gasped. He could not believe what he heard.

"Yes, Jacob. You had a twin sister," she revealed. "You came out two minutes after her. I dealt with you. After cutting the umbilical cord I cleaned you off and made sure you took your first breath and wrapped you in a warm towel. I had to leave your sister with Iris. That turned out exactly how I expected. A disaster. When I returned to the room, Iris was passed out. The baby lay on the bed next to her, covered with a pillow. She was blue. She couldn't be saved."

Braun interrupted. "Did Iris kill her?"

"I won't speculate, but let's just say she didn't want either baby. If I would have left Jacob with her, he would have suffered the same fate. I'm sure of it. Both babies were extremely frail. A little over two pounds is all. She may not have survived anyway."

"I had a sister. Goddamn it! I cannot believe this," he yelled. "Why didn't anyone ever tell me?"

"What good would it have done, Jacob? My focus was on you. Only you. Saving your life. Keeping you as my own," she confessed. "I knew Iris would've never raised you."

"Where was your mother, Rose?" Braun asked.

"Out of the way," she said. "I told her the baby girl didn't survive the birth. She didn't need to know the truth."

"What did you do with the body?" Braun pressed.

"I went straight to the basement. I placed the baby in one of dad's boot boxes," she stoically explained. "Then, I put her and the box in a plastic bag. I placed everything into a larger plastic bag and sealed it."

"And then buried her, I assume?"

"In the pen, right next to this silo," she pointed. "Braun, you are sitting twenty-five feet from her."

"Did Iris have any other children?" Jacob compelled an answer. "Were there more?"

Aunt Rose hesitated, but knew she had to give Jacob something to calm his anger.

"Iris had been pregnant two other times, some years before you were born," she revealed. "I aborted both pregnancies. Right here, on the farm."

"I guess I should be thankful," he pondered. "That woman had no right to be a mother."

"She wasn't a mother, Jacob," Aunt Rose quickly interjected. "I was your mother. Iris could have never raised a child. Never. I knew that."

"Who was the father of the baby girl and Jacob, Rose?" Braun confronted.

Rose hesitated. She looked up and outward, across the Weaver's farm land. She shook her head side to side. Bowed her head. Rose's strained expression broke through her usual calm façade. She had a look of overdue acquiescence. As if she was in a confessional booth, releasing a lifetime of guilt off her shoulders. Braun saw how difficult it was for Rose to tell the entire truth. Some pain she held onto was greater than others. He was amazed how her mind resisted. Holding onto the excruciating secrets that tortured her for decades. Was it a defense mechanism? What made the soul grip so tightly onto experiences that only destroy? Aren't they just words? Or is the revelation of her guilt too crushing? Had all the lies become so deeply embedded into her soul, revealing them was worse than keeping them hidden?

"Jacob. I'm not sure if you are prepared for what I am about to tell you," she said. "This is a chance for you to leave and allow me to speak to Detective Braun, alone."

"No. No. I need to listen," he answered. "I need to hear it."

"You do know your father," she said. "You came face to face with him many times."

"That's not possible," he said. "I would have known."

"It is just not that simple."

"I am telling you," he grimaced. "I definitely would have known."

"It's Wyatt."

"Wyatt is not my father." Jacob didn't want to know the truth.

"Wyatt is your father."

"I won't accept that."

Jacob and Braun stirred, while Rose became silent. She knew there was no reason to argue the fact. Wyatt was dead. Jacob spun around, in a full circle, as if he needed to find an escape from this nightmare. Braun moved in closer to the silo. Jacob now thought, *did I kill my own father?*

"Hard to hear, I know," she agreed. "Believe me, it's even harder to finally tell you."

Jacob sat quiet. He looked straight down at the ground. It was as if he felt guilty simply for being part of the Weaver family. The name alone made him sick to his stomach. Here was a man that came and went from the farm, never once giving a hint that he was Jacob's biological father. Never once showing a sign of any emotional bond.

Braun flipped open his phone and made a call. He needed someone with more training than him to try and talk Rose from this proverbial ledge. He contacted a trained negotiator that had once helped him with a deteriorating hostage situation, but he knew this was different. Rose was not a hostage, taken within the context of the training manual. In a way, she was her own hostage. Fighting with her own inner turmoil. Jacob's arrest had opened Pandora's Box. There would be no way to stuff her life's chaos back in. Rose knew all about the three strikes law and knew Jacob was facing a fate he had not been able to grasp. A life sentence? She couldn't endure such a reality. Jacob was the only living thing she loved.

"Who did you call, Detective?" Rose demanded. "I know you called somebody to come out here."

"Somebody that is smarter than me to talk you down from there, Rose," he told her. "She is a good woman. She will know how to help you."

"Braun, if I see a car come up that driveway...."

He got her message and got back on his phone, quickly, and called off the negotiator.

"What about Iris?" Jacob asked.

"What do you mean?"

"The problems with you and Iris and Grandpa?"

"Iris and I handled our issues with Grandpa differently," she began. "We lived a very tough life. It wasn't easy for her."

"Issues?" Braun pressed. "Sounds like more than issues, Rose."

"Abuse, Detective," she snapped. "There was no time for us to be kids. We didn't know what it was like to be little girls. He made Grandma cut our hair short. We didn't even look like girls. He worked us like the other farmers worked their sons. Went to school when we could, but that wasn't very often. Grandma got us books. As many as possible.

When he got mad at us, we were put in the silo. Sometimes we were put in there together and sometimes we were put in there alone. It was the darkness and the cold. Those terrible smells. Iris was younger than me. She was afraid. She couldn't handle it. If we were in there together, I kept her occupied. We didn't know when he would let us out. We were trapped. Like animals. And when he did let us out, he put us back to work. I learned what control meant. I learned that I would someday be the one in control. I was determined to be on top of that silo, not inside of it. I found comfort there. On top. Looking out over the land that I would someday control. The Weaver family farm would be mine. Just like you were going to be mine, Jacob, my son. My special son."

"So, this went on for years?" Braun explored.

"You become numb to it. Seemed like there was no way out. Nowhere to run. Why didn't I leave? Escape everything? Those are the questions that are bouncing around in your head, right Braun? Sounds so easy. Iris escaped within her drinking and drugs. I escaped within my books. Within my gradual, and purposeful, move to take control of every situation in my life. Whenever I sat alone inside that dark, musty silo, I told myself I would survive. I would be the master of my own fate."

"And what about Iris?"

"Crack. And alcohol," she said. "Mix that with her desperation, her belief at times that her life was crashing in on her if she didn't get money, or a car, or the drugs, or a place to sleep. She always came back to the farm. What some people will do when they are reduced to nothing. When self-loathing controls your every thought."

"What about those pregnancies? The abortions?" Jacob pressed. "Who was the father?"

"I cannot talk about that. I will not speak those ugly words," she confessed.

"Why?" Braun confronted. "If now is not the time, when will there ever be another time?"

"There won't!" she barked. "Her pregnancies are between her, the father and God. All I could do for her, at the time, was eliminate the problem. I made her problems go away. That was how I kept control of the hand dealt to her. Abuse is a terrible thing."

"She was like an animal," Jacob shouted to the sky. "Is that what you're saying?"

"Who was the animal?" Braun challenged. "She was extremely vulnerable in her condition. What about him? Where is his accountability in all of this?"

"She could have resisted, Detective," Rose demanded. "She was an adult. I'm not letting her off the hook so easily. She chose drugs and alcohol as her escape. Those were her choices."

"But she had to have suffered that kind of abuse when she was young," Braun speculated. "It is highly unlikely that he was able to manipulate a grown woman. His own daughter? To engage in something this heinous."

A dark stillness overcame Aunt Rose. She recognized Braun's grim insinuation.

"I never said it was my father, Braun," she chastised. "Never put thoughts in Jacob's head, or words in my mouth. You have no right."

Braun had undeniably struck a raw nerve. He had seemingly pulled the ugly truth out of Rose. This was an open and enduring wound. A vicious and a violent truth, she had promised she would take to her grave. Iris was not strong enough to resist the devil's hand. Rose shifted her now uncomfortable body. The top of the silo seemed to be getting smaller and smaller, psychologically shrinking beneath her unsteady feet.

"Rose!" Braun shouted. "Did you suffer the same fate as Iris?"

Nothing was heard but painful silence. Braun was able to hear his own heartbeat. *Was Grandpa truly the father of Iris' aborted babies?* He knew Rose would never reveal that dark secret.

"Isn't now the time to explain completely what happened to you girls," he said. "Your father is dead. So is your mother. They cannot reach you."

"The power of their memory can reach me. I will not make this about me," she shouted back at Braun. "There are things I will take to my grave. I must. I've chosen my own path. Cops always have to have a victim. I won't be your victim."

"Why? Why take the pain with you?" he stated. "Let it go. Free your soul."

"I said no. There must be something left that I can still control," she demanded. "As foolish as that might sound, if I speak of those unspeakable acts, I have given all that I have to give. I need some power to hold on to. You cannot have it. My personal shame, no matter how excruciating, is mine. I choose to live and die with it."

"Iris?" he asked. "What about Iris?"

"All I will tell you is that she and I spoke about it," she said. "Our secret was a brittle bond between us. What happened in that silo stays in that silo. All the guilt and pain. It brought us closer, in some ways, but it also tore us apart. Her childhood was haunted by things that happened."

"But, what about…"

"Stop…right…there, Braun," Rose interrupted. "No more. I won't speak of this any longer."

Braun stared up to the top of the silo. He watched her furtive movements. Waiting.

"That man never considered us his daughters," Rose said. "My father. Iris' father. He got exactly what he deserved."

"Where's Iris?" Braun pressured. He knew Rose held tightly to this secret. One she now knew was time to reveal. "Iris hasn't been missing for all these years, has she?"

TWELVE

NIGHTFALL WAS SETTING IN. Rose was exhausted. Her silence now spoke volumes about her stamina. She had shared secrets that had slept for decades. Draining on an aging mind and body. Her revelations were an explosion of guilt. But regret? He was not so sure. Braun was at the point where unraveling those mysteries were imminent. These phenomena led them both in opposite directions. Braun thought of the future. What would happen to Jacob? Where would this all lead? For Rose, she thought about the past. Where had she been? Why did it have to be?

"Rose?" he interrupted her distant gaze. "Iris?"

"I know. I know."

"So, can you talk to Iris? Can I talk to her?" he tested. "We will let her explain what happened to her as a child. She can determine her own fate, Rose."

"She is not able to determine her own fate, Detective," she answered, "but, I think you know that."

"Where's Iris, Aunt Rose?" Jacob pressured her for the answer.

"She's gone, Jacob!"

"Where has she gone? You must know."

"She's gone, forever," she confessed. "Now you know the truth. She has been dead for many years."

Jacob abruptly jumped to his feet and walked in circles, to the left and back to the right. As if he had nowhere to escape. It was like he was trapped in the silo again. He wasn't certain if he wanted to know the rest of the truth. Honesty was becoming another form of agony. Perhaps, living without knowing was easier.

"How?" Braun questioned. "This can't end here, Rose. We need to finish this and find out the whole truth."

"And I have wondered where she was since I was fifteen," he said, feeling foolish. "She has been dead for all these years?"

"What happened to her?" Braun demanded. He had to get it all for Jacob.

Rose stood and carefully walked around to the opposite side of the silo. Braun had lost direct line of sight. He didn't try to walk around to the other side of the silo, because the pen's fence blocked his pathway. He waited. Braun wasn't sure what would happen next. He waited longer. Then, she appeared again after making a full circle around the top of the silo. She sat back down on the edge, dangling her legs, like a child on a tall stool.

"Jacob was about to turn sixteen," she described. "That's a very special time for a son."

"The son Iris ignored since the day he was born?" He knew his question would bring anger.

"Jacob was my son!" Rose shouted. Her voice pierced the country sky. "My son, Braun. My son! No one else can claim him. Especially, not her. Not Iris. I won't allow it."

"Iris gave birth to Jacob."

"Giving birth is easy, Detective. Any woman can have a baby. Having a child does not make you a mother," she yelled. "Can't anyone understand that? Look at what she did to her first two babies. To his sister. What I did to them, because of her. I took care of Jacob since the day he was born. I saved him from her. He is mine. And that is why, to this very day, he still considers me his mother. Don't you, Jacob? I allowed you to call me Aunt Rose, so you wouldn't be confused. That is all. I was protecting him, Braun."

"Why didn't she want me dead, too?" Jacob questioned. "Why not abort me? Why let me live?"

"Jacob. Listen to what you are saying," Rose laughed out of irony. "Don't you understand what I am telling you? She did not want you. She wasn't even aware she was pregnant. She wanted you dead. Just like the first two. Just like your sister. She wanted me to kill you, too. She did not want you, Son."

"Then why am I here?"

"Because I wanted you, Jacob," she explained. "I was in control of your fate. I put my foot down. It was my decision. My plan. She wouldn't even hold you. Wouldn't touch you, Jacob. She would not even look into your sweet face. She turned her head. She rejected you."

"But you wouldn't let him die," Braun said. "Jacob was different?"

"He was as helpless as anything I had ever seen. I could have killed him for Iris in an instant," she admitted. "That's what she wanted. Just like his sister."

"You let me live," Jacob realized. "Without you, I wouldn't be here."

"I immediately put you in one of Grandpa's old boot boxes to carry you around," she explained. "Grandma was so shocked you survived. She could not believe how small you were."

"What did Iris do?"

"She was furious with me," she answered. "As if letting you live made her feel guilty. Made her feel ashamed that she had no love for you. No bond. She saw her life imploding right in front of her eyes. You would have ruined her life as she knew it. You would've been an extra burden on her already chaotic life. She told me that you were mine. She demanded I take you. It is exactly what I was planning all along. I was just caught off guard that it was all happening so quickly. She didn't know she was pregnant. I was stunned she was giving birth."

"What about Wyatt?" he asked. "Did Wyatt know I was his son?"

"Of course he knew," Rose revealed.

Braun's pressure was mounting. "Where is Iris? Now is the time to tell me."

"She's here, Detective," she confessed. "By the silo."

Braun stood and walked to the wooden fence, surrounding the pen, knowing he was staring into a burial ground. "She came to the farm," Rose clarified. "All alone."

"Alone?" Braun questioned. "No Wyatt this time?"

"No Wyatt," she said. "Which was quite annoying for me."

"Why did she come home alone this time?"

"She said she had broken things off with Wyatt. He was a bastard according to her," Rose laughed. "He was the bastard? Can you believe the gall? After what she had put everybody through for years? Two abortions. Jacob. A child she literally discarded like garbage. I knew why she came back."

He let her continue without interruption.

"What do all addicts want?" Rose lectured. "Money. A place to sleep. Take advantage. You know what it's like to be a drunk, right Braun?"

"This isn't about me, Rose," he reminded. "This is about you. About Iris. About Jacob."

"But it was about you, Braun, a long time ago when Jacob ran away from this farm," she accused. "Jacob was only twelve. You brought him back to us. You remember me. You thought I was his mother. Rosemary Weaver. I smelled the booze on your breath. I told you it would be best to just leave him with me and not to ask too many questions. Not to dig too deeply into my family. Questions would have led to problems for me and the farm. You didn't push it, did you Braun? Looking back, you let Jacob down. You didn't ask any questions. You weighed your options. In return, I didn't call your supervisor about the booze on your breath. It worked out for both of us."

Braun's blood pressure rose. His silence revealed his guilt. Guilt had a way of doing that to a man. Braun was determined to make it right now, for Jacob. Braun had to keep the focus on Rose and her crimes. His remorse for his own past behaviors would be dealt with in his own way. *I must keep the focus on Rose.*

"Why were you so angry Wyatt didn't show up with Iris?"

"Let your imagination work for you, Detective," she said. "After all, you are a man. You know what men want."

"You and Wyatt?"

"Wyatt wasn't there just to be with Iris," she explained. "We were having a longtime affair. When she was stoned or drunk, which was most of the time, he and I were finding time for each other. It wasn't difficult to pull off. He had lost all feelings for Iris. It was Wyatt and me who planned her pregnancy."

"Say that again."

"I know, it sounds crazy," she said, "but I was never able to have kids. And I knew it. I will admit that it angered me that a woman like Iris could have children whenever she wanted. Whenever she had sex with a man. What a waste. Wyatt knew I wanted a child. I needed a child. How could he give me one? I knew exactly how."

"Through Iris?"

"Why not?"

"You knew she wouldn't agree to keep the baby." Braun assumed. "She would want to get rid of it. Like the others."

"That is exactly what I planned," she revealed. "I would vehemently refuse to abort a third child for her. For her health. Where else was she going to go for an abortion? To a legitimate doctor? Hospital? A drug addict does not risk going to any medical facility. So, Iris has Wyatt's baby and the next best thing is that I deliver it, keep it, knowing she would totally reject it. She depended on me to clean up her messes. They all did."

"So, you didn't have to worry about an abortion."

"I got lucky, if that's how you want to look at it," she admitted. "She was so messed up. Didn't even know she was pregnant. It happens. Hard to believe, but it does happen."

"So, she thought Wyatt got her pregnant accidentally?"

"She was so naïve," Rose said. "Being stoned all the time will make you that way."

"How did you kill her?"

"She decided to up and leave right before Jacob's birthday," she seethed. "Grandpa had given her more money, the day before. He wanted her out. We were upstairs in her bedroom. She was getting her bags together. I confronted her. I told her that she had been a failure her whole life. She said, 'Anybody who sleeps with her sister's man was the one who was a failure.' I don't know if Wyatt confided in her, or if she just figured it out. She didn't give a damn about the sex. Sex meant nothing to her. I don't think she ever cared who Wyatt slept with. But it was her way of telling me that she knew what I had done. She walked out of her bedroom and turned toward me at the top of the stairs. I was getting angrier and angrier with her tone. I had raised Jacob for fifteen years, and I still had to deal with that bitch. I yelled at her that she was a loser again and again and again. I wanted it to sink in. I wanted it to hurt."

Rose stood up and began to pace on top of the silo, nearly losing her balance. Struggling with releasing her crimes.

"Why hurt her after all those years?"

"She deserved it. And she took the bait."

"Were your parents gone?"

"Yes. She always tried to get out of town without them knowing," she said. "Mother was at church. Dad was in town at the hardware store. They wouldn't be home for quite a while. I knew that. Iris knew that. That is when she liked to just disappear."

"How did the fight end?"

"With her tumbling head first down the stairs, that's how," she confessed.

"You pushed her down the stairs?"

"Iris caused her own death, Braun. Remember that. She got so mad with me when I told her I didn't plan on stopping what was going on between me and Wyatt. She was facing me. She was yelling at me. She was calling me a whore. I'm the whore? I could feel her spit spraying in my face. I instantly reacted. I shoved her as hard as I could. She flew backwards down the stairs. They are old and very solid, oak stairs. I heard her head crack more than once on the way down. Oak is not very forgiving, Detective. When she landed at the bottom, she struck the back of her head on the corner of the baseboard that stuck out. The baseboard was made of that same hard oak. I knew it broke her skull, or neck, or both. She was definitely dead. There was no doubt about that."

"You sound so matter of fact. Did you plan on killing her at some point in time, or was it a last second decision?" he probed.

"I see what you want to know, Braun," she smirked. "Was it premeditated?"

"There's no remorse? She was your sister. You both suffered when you were kids," he said. "She was younger than you. You said you tried to protect her when she was having a hard time dealing with abuse."

"Do I wish she hadn't forced me to do what I had to do?" she pondered with self-centered hindsight.

"She forced you to kill her? Is that what you're telling me?"

"I wish people didn't do lots of things to get themselves in a mess like she did."

"So, her death was her fault?"

"Fault? Is that the question that is so important? Now? After all these years. One person destroys the lives of everyone around her. I can't help it that she was my sister. You think she is the victim here? Drugs. Alcohol. Neglect. She was always the victim," she ranted. "Damn it, Braun, can't you see her death was her own fault. I'm the one that did it, sure. I shoved her. I caused her to fall down those stairs. I know I killed her. But she killed herself that day as far as I'm concerned. She brought it upon herself. Things are never so black and white. There are reasons why bad things happen. You should know that better than anybody."

THIRTEEN

BRAUN UNDERSTOOD Rose's insinuation. He looked back all those years with guilt. It was hard to accept that his own drinking problem caused people pain, and not just Jacob. If Braun would have placed Jacob's well-being above his own desire to block out the haunting memories of Vietnam, where would Jacob be today? Which direction would Jacob's life have gone? Certainly not facing a life sentence in prison. Jacob was only a child of twelve when he ran away and Braun now felt he had let him down. Jacob had nowhere to go. He was crying out for help. Braun finally realized, all these years later, he could have impacted Jacob's direction in life. Braun also knew that he needed to make amends. Somehow. Some way. Braun had come to know that Jacob was sheltered from the whole truth. He had built his own narrative of his upbringing, his brain trying to reduce the sting. A narrative that was often methodically shaped, and twisted, for him, but not by him. Braun pushed Rose for more.

"Jacob confessed to me that he killed Wyatt," Braun pursued. "Jacob tried to take the blame. He wants to take responsibility for killing him. But, he's not to blame. Is he, Rose?"

"Jacob couldn't kill a fly," she said. "You have already talked to Jacob enough to know he hasn't a violent bone in his body, Detective. I'm sure he told you the story of the chicken. It was laughable at the time. Jacob could not have killed Wyatt. He may think he did. The power of guilt can be overwhelming in a young man. All the confusion, the darkness, and the blood. Jacob's blood. Wyatt's blood. The mind has a defense mechanism for devising a truth that simply does not exist."

"Why did Wyatt have to die?"

"Because he would not let it go," she specified.

Braun noticed that Rose almost slipped off the edge of the silo, gaining her balance at the last moment. Whatever core strength she once had, it was disintegrating.

"Come down from there, Rose," Braun tried persuading. "Let's finish this down here. For Jacob's sake."

"Wyatt had to come back. He couldn't leave well enough alone. After he got released from jail. He had to return to the farm. Back to the chaos. He came back for my sister, his cocaine sniffing partner, but I was the one he truly loved. Even if he wouldn't say it. He came back so he could keep screwing me. He said that I was the stable one. He knew that, but the drugs kept him going back to Iris. I was the one he made promises to. I was the one he fathered Jacob for. But he made a fatal mistake, returning to the farm and trying to reveal my secrets. To what end? For who? For her? The woman that ruined our lives?"

"What did you do to him, Rose?" Braun pressed.

"All those months after I killed Iris," she said, "Wyatt showing up only made things worse. He had been in jail for a long time right before that. But here he came. Unannounced. I heard his motorcycle coming up the gravel drive. As much as I loved him at one time, everything had changed after what happened to Iris. I still had Jacob. That is all I cared about. A young man now. He was now starting to drive. Grandpa gave in to my request, or should I say demand. I wanted Jacob to get the car Iris had been driving all those years. He gave in. Jacob now had some freedom. A real chance. To get away from the farm. The root of our problems, Iris, was taken care of. Her mess was cleaned up. He could get away from the years of violence and that lingering smell of death."

"Did you allow Wyatt in?"

"I did allow him in," she said. "What else could I do at that point? I wanted him to stay calm. I knew why he was there. I knew this could explode into something bad at any moment."

"Did it blow up?"

"Not right away," she said. "We tried to talk to him."

"Who's we?"

"All of us at first. Even Grandpa spoke up," she explained. "You know, trying to calm Wyatt down. You must know by now that Grandma and Grandpa only knew what I told them. That Iris was gone. That she had left again. On her own. They had no clue they could see her burial ground from their living room window."

"What about Grandpa's car?" Braun probed. "It was still at the farm, right? She always took his car."

"I made up a cover story," she said. "That Iris got angry and wanted to leave. I wouldn't let her have the car keys. She took a stand and told me I would have to drive her to the bus station. Which I told them that I did. I even bought a ticket to Kentucky, in her name. I lied to cover my tracks. They believed anything I told them."

"So, wouldn't Wyatt have wondered where she was, since the car was still at the farm? The car she always drove."

"It made him more than wonder," she said. "It made him suspicious. It made him furious at me. It made him confront all of us."

Rose was becoming livid, while retelling the story. The thought of Wyatt brought out visible anger in her face. Braun could hear the contempt in her voice, as she recalled Wyatt's lack of loyalty to her. After their most intimate moments and their most intimate plans, her resentment was boiling to the top. Rose was now exposing the true level of her emotional wounds from the depth of his betrayal.

"I didn't want Jacob to get involved, but he did anyway when he followed Wyatt out of the house that night," she emphasized. "I had to think of a way to intervene. Jacob was completely convinced Iris had left the farm again, left him again. Because, that was Iris. That is who she was. He wouldn't have suspected anything different."

"But, Wyatt did?"

"Of course he did. Because of his suspicion, Wyatt gave me no choice," she rationalized. "People never give me a choice. He gave me no other option, Braun. Wyatt dug his own grave the night he showed up at my front door."

Rose's mental health was deteriorating right in front of Braun's eyes. The release of so much pent-up anger was making her delirious. Braun could tell that Rose felt no sense of responsibility for Iris and Wyatt's deaths. In her mind, both had betrayed her in their own separate ways. She was staring out across the fields, in a trance, talking non-stop about how it happened. Braun believed this was her way of absolving Jacob of any guilt for Wyatt's death.

"Wyatt went outside and started looking around," she continued. "You know, snooping around. I knew what he was up to. I watched from the window. Jacob had been out on the porch watching him as well. Then, I saw Wyatt heading toward the barn and the silo. Walking straight toward Iris' grave. Within minutes I saw Jacob following. Jacob thought he could convince Wyatt to leave this all alone. That he was getting paranoid about her disappearance. He told him that Iris would come back when she was damn good and ready."

"Like a hundred times before?"

"Like a thousand times before."

"So, I went outside. I did not trust Wyatt alone with Jacob," she said.

"He and Jacob were now standing by the silo. Close to Iris' grave. Wyatt was smoking a cigarette and talking to Jacob. He seemed very angry still."

"Did you ever see him pull a knife on Jacob?"

"Actually, pull it on Jacob?" she thought back. "Threaten him with it? He was angry, but even Wyatt knew that Jacob would have had nothing to do with the disappearance of Iris. I did see Wyatt take his knife from the sheath. In a way, he just used it when he talked. Like some people use their hands, you know. I saw him stabbing the blade into a wooden fence post. Next to the silo. Just a nervous habit. When he talked. Relieving frustration."

"What was Wyatt saying to Jacob?" Braun asked. "Were you ever close enough to hear?"

"I finally got close enough," she said. "But I was standing behind the silo. They couldn't see me. Not even Jacob knew I was there."

"Did he threaten Jacob?"

"He was fuming. That is all I can say about that," she said. "Was he threatening Jacob? I don't know, but he was beginning to threaten me."

"He threatened you? How?" he asked for clarification. "It was still very dark, and you were behind the silo, right? Did he even know you were there?"

I heard him telling Jacob, 'I'm going to search this entire goddamn farm for Iris,' and he said he was going to start right then. Right there. Right by the silo. He was going to find a shovel and start digging."

"So, he was drawn to the silo and that muddy pen next to it?"

"Yes. And I couldn't have that," she admitted. "I could not have him digging around in that pen. Disturbing their graves."

"And..."

"And I came from around the back of the silo. There was a garden hoe there, leaning against the side of the fence."

"It wasn't a shovel?" Braun questioned. "Jacob said it was a shovel."

"Jacob is wrong. He doesn't remember," she said. "All of what happened that night to Jacob was a blur. Obviously, he has false memories. He is trying to take a puzzle with missing pieces and make them fit. It cannot be done, Braun. This is all just displaced guilt for him being there. Following Wyatt around. He feels responsible. Wants to take the blame for what happened that night. For what I did."

"Did Jacob stab Wyatt?"

"I didn't see Jacob stab Wyatt. It was too dark," she recalled. "For God sakes, there is no way Jacob could stab someone. Not on purpose."

"I always thought I stabbed him," Jacob admitted. "While we struggled."

"I let you believe it, Jacob. I was the one that grabbed the hoe and came up behind Wyatt. He didn't notice me until it was too late. Like I said, it was pitch black," she repeated. "There was no lighting. I swung as hard as I could and struck Wyatt in the back of the head with that iron brace on the back of the hoe. I heard his skull crack. It was loud. Sounded like a tree branch snapping. It sounded just like Iris' head."

"That is when Jacob realized you had struck Wyatt?"

"Yes."

"What happened next?"

"Wyatt was still holding the knife as he was falling," she described. "Jacob reached out for Wyatt as he fell. I think he was trying to catch him. Jacob accidentally grabbed the blade of the knife. This knocked the knife from Wyatt's hand, but it dropped to the ground, and buried in the mud. The handle was down and the blade up."

"So, you're saying the blade was sticking straight up in the air now?"

Braun confirmed.

"That's exactly what I'm saying."

"And Wyatt fell on the knife?"

"And it buried right into the side of his body...under his ribcage."

"Jacob said he remembered Wyatt standing up, laughing about the fight between them. Even lighting another cigarette?"

"That isn't what happened, Detective," she smirked at the notion. "Jacob is mixing and matching different things that may have happened. Wyatt did slowly make it to his feet. He was swaying. Off balance. He could barely stand. He looked down. That is when he said, 'You got me Jacob.'"

"So, Wyatt was blaming Jacob. He thought Jacob had stabbed him?"

"Wyatt was completely dazed and groggy," she went on. "He thought Jacob was to blame. Jacob was only protecting himself. Wyatt may have thought Jacob stabbed him somehow, but that is because he was in shock. He was losing blood. He was delirious. He didn't know I was even there. His knife was sticking out of his body. I'm sure his skull was fractured from the sound of that metal hoe. But Wyatt did get back up to his feet. I was shocked with his head injury. He had to be bleeding out."

"What did he do next?"

"Wyatt put his hand against the silo and tried to steady himself. Stood there looking down at the knife sticking out of his body," she described. "Jacob's hand was bleeding terribly from grabbing the blade of the knife. I told him, 'Get out of here Jacob,' and Wyatt slowly turned toward me when he heard my voice. Our eyes met just for a moment. His face was covered in blood. I don't know how he was still standing."

"Did he speak to you, Rose?"

"I didn't give him the chance," she said. "I swung the hoe as hard as I could again and struck him on the side of his head."

"Which side?"

"The left. Yes, the left side. By his temple."

Braun wanted Rose to give him specific details of the injury, so he could compare her confession to the evidence. The fractured skull of Wyatt's body should reveal a large crack on the left side.

"This time you knew?"

"I knew it was crushed bone. Wyatt slumped down into the mud," she said. "He never moved again. I knew he was dead."

"Was Jacob gone by now?"

"He went back to the house to wrap up the cut to this hand," she said, "and I told him to get his ass down to Ronnie's place."

"Then what?"

"I cleaned up Wyatt's mess," she said so matter-of-fact, as if he had brought all of this upon himself. She didn't have it in her heart to take responsibility for her lover's death.

"You are telling me that you got rid of Wyatt's body and his motorcycle all by yourself?"

"When you find it, you will see that it was not that difficult, Detective," she grinned. "When you live on a farm, you have many options."

FOURTEEN

ROSE HAD UNVEILED DEADLY sins she had committed on the Weaver family farm dating back many years. Braun wondered where it would end. Revelations brought more suspicion. Suspicion brought more questions. When did the killing begin? He had never witnessed anything like this in his career. She confessed to the murder of both Wyatt and Iris. Yet, she offered nothing regarding the death of her father. Jacob suspected his grandmother of killing him, but apparently Rose never thought Jacob would speak of his death to Braun. Aunt Rose knew Jacob overheard her conversation with her mother to cover it up if anyone outside the family raised questions. His death was only seven years ago, and Jacob was sure it was not accidental.

Braun could not let those questions go unanswered. For whatever reason, Rose wanted to avoid the question of her father's death. And it was the one, and only one, death that Jacob believed was caused by his grandmother. Braun wasn't convinced.

"How did your mother deal with murdering her own husband, Rose?" he bluntly accused.

"Detective Braun. That is such a loaded question," she scoffed. "You are so gifted at casually drawing me in. Putting your suspicions right smack in the middle of the question. The methods you use to insinuate, alluding to only partial truths. Then, you force a response that gets right down to the bottom of the whole truth. I wondered when you would get to my father's unfortunate demise."

"All I want is the undeniable truth," he said. "Jacob already told me about your mother giving him an overdose of morphine. That's murder, Rose."

"Insinuations, Braun. Partial truths."

"Partial?"

"I figured he presented that scenario to you," she said. "Again, life is exactly how one chooses to perceive it. How one assumes what has happened, instead of knows what has happened. You know what I mean, Detective. Is the glass half empty or half full? I'm sure it has been difficult for Jacob to believe what he believes. About his grandmother, I mean."

"He perceived his death as intentional. Was it intentional or accidental?"

"Smooth move. Offer me two answers, in which both places culpability on my mother," she smirked. "It's like me asking, when did you stop beating your wife, Braun? Either answer you are confessing to wrongdoing."

"Are you saying Jacob is lying about what he heard?" Braun probed. "Your sense of truth is quite malleable, Rose. Is there another form of truth I need to know about?"

"Two people perceive things very differently," she said. "Remember, Jacob saw absolutely nothing. He never witnessed a crime. He only pieced things together. Made assumptions. Assumptions can turn out to bite you in the butt. Like I said before, people try very hard to make puzzle pieces fit in places they just won't. Jacob tried to listen in on a private conversation. When he did that, he heard what he wanted to hear. He turned out to be very, very wrong."

"What did he get wrong?"

"The overdose didn't kill him," she admitted. "My father was a dying man, Braun. Leading up to his death my father began to talk. All those years of silence, now he wanted to ramble on. Clear his conscience. Not always willingly, either. His mind wandered. He spoke in fragments. Powerful drugs will do that to a sick man. He often hallucinated. Recollections came out in words he never realized he was speaking. But he did apologize to her."

"For what?"

"How he was after the war. The problems on the farm. Why he hated her church so much."

"That sounds harmless," he said. "Isn't it normal to want forgiveness when you are dying? A man searching for absolution from those he hurt so badly?"

"He told her that he was remorseful about us girls," Rose explained. "What he had done to us. And for causing Iris to turn to drugs and alcohol. Her trying to escape from everything in her life. From Mother and the farm. From the church."

"And Iris' abortions?"

"My mother never spoke a single word of them."

"But you believe she knew?"

"I assume she knew."

Rose hesitated. Her abrupt silence concerned Braun. Was she done talking? He had to keep her talking. He needed to convince her to come down from the silo.

"Rose...stay with me, Rose."

"She came out of his room that afternoon. He had been in a lot of pain. She seemed withdrawn and stern. Seemed unsympathetic," she recalled. "Mother called out for me. Very matter-of-factly. No emotion."

"What did she tell you?"

"That she gave him an overdose of morphine," she said. "That she was done with him. She had to stop the suffering."

"Who's suffering? His?"

"Oh no...," she paused. "I believe she was speaking of her own suffering."

Braun did not speak. He knew Rose would finish, now, in her own time. He allowed her hesitancy.

"I went into the bedroom and he was still alive," she said. "His breathing was shallow. He was at the end. He had spoken his last words of regret. I grabbed his nose and squeezed, covering his mouth. With all my weight I leaned over him and pushed. I pushed. I was lying on top of him now. I pushed until any sign of life ceased. His weakened struggle came to an end. Hardly gave any resistance. I was too strong for him. I always was."

"You murdered him?"

"He killed himself, as far as I'm concerned. I just physically ended it for him. For her," she confessed. "I didn't want the overdose to be the cause of his death. I refused to let him die on his own. For what he did. To us. He could have kept his mouth shut for her. He didn't have to tell her a thing. He could have taken his nasty secrets to his grave. But, like many others before him, he had to force his pain and guilt onto the living. As if he thought someone would forgive what he had done. No forgiveness from me. He was asking to be killed."

"So, again, his murder was his own fault?"

"Your questions are so naive, as if there is no process," she grinned. "Without any understanding of the complexities of murder. So black and white, Detective. Can't you see that killing someone is a difficult decision? There is a thought process that goes into it for me. It is not as easy as you may think. It's learned over time. You get better with the next one. There are decisions. Like how? Like when?"

"So, you were planning on eventually killing your father, is that it?" he asked, "for what he did to you and Iris?"

"Of course," she said. "Opportunity knocks but once. This opportunity banged on my door loudly that day. I had to take it. My mother tried, but was too weak. I took care of it for her. Just like I took care of everything. For everybody, on this farm. She is not to blame."

Rose became eerily quiet. She was fatigued with the release of such intense revelations. She had confessed to killing three people. Braun saw her wearing down. She was giving up the fight. Somehow, deep down, Braun did not believe that was all. Perhaps, it was enough though. There are times when you simply cannot push for every ounce of information. You often take what you can get and move on.

Rose had reached her limit. Braun had no control of her physically, or mentally. Her legs dangled over the edge of the silo. He waited for a sign. Rose was not coming down on her own volition. There were many decisions to be made. There was a need to call for a team of crime scene technicians. There would be a need for someone to search and locate the bodies. Dig up the graves. If bodies or bones were found, the coroner would be summoned. The entire farm would be secured and tightly sealed as an active crime scene. Braun knew the hard work had not even begun.

"Detective Braun!"

He could tell she was about to make an announcement. *Where will we go from here?*

"I'm here, Rose."

"I need Jacob to leave right now."

"Why?"

"I need to talk to you alone," she demanded. "Get Jacob out of my sight."

"I'm not going anywhere, Aunt Rose," Jacob said. "I'm not leaving here without you."

"Detective Braun," she replied. "Please get Jacob out of here."

"I'll put him in my car."

"Just get him out of my sight," she said. "Go on, Jacob."

He did as he was told. Like always. Still in the psychological grasp of his aunt and the power she held over him all his life.

"I will be over there shortly, Jacob. When I'm done here with Rose I will come and speak to you about what is next."

Jacob walked reluctantly to the car, anticipating the worst. Now, he felt guilty for ever speaking to Braun about his life. Jacob could still see the barn and the silo from the car, but he could not see the backside of the silo. Therefore, he could not actually see Aunt Rose. She knew that. Rose was smart. She knew exactly what she was doing.

"I have some instructions for you, Detective. It is very important that you listen closely to everything I say."

"I'm listening, Rose."

"You have treated Jacob with respect. That is something I cannot say for all the other adults in his life. And that includes me. You have also treated me with respect. I have a list of demands."

"Talk to me."

"They are more like steps for you to take to make wrapping this all up much easier. I can only help you to a certain degree," she said. Rose froze in thought. "That is absolutely beautiful, isn't it?"

She stopped speaking and fell deep into thought. As if she was ruminating about the past.

"Say that again, Rose. I didn't catch what you said."

"I said it is absolutely beautiful."

"What's beautiful?"

"Look at the sunset, Detective," she pointed.

Braun looked to the west. The sun had turned a pigeon-blood red.

"When that sunlight bounces off the fields it is a beautiful sight to see," she offered. "This farm was mine, Detective. I kept it together. I lived here my whole life. I took care of my parents. The farm. I never wanted for anything more. I was born to be who I am. The outside world offered me nothing. I took care of everybody and everything within my circle."

"You took a lot upon your own shoulders, Rose," he said. "That kind of dedication can be overwhelming."

"Have you ever read, *Light in August*?" she asked.

"I haven't."

"Faulkner. You should read it," she said. "That deep red ball of fire to the west belongs to all of us. It is my light. It is your light, too. It gives what it can give for the day...and then it sets. Only to return and give us more. Lena Grove appreciated that light."

"Lena Grove?"

"She is an important character in that book. Lena knew her destiny. There was no question the direction she was going to take in her life."

"What was her destiny?"

"A family. A husband. A legitimate child," she said. "Not unlike the path I've tried to forge."

"You still have Jacob."

"Do you know what Faulkner said about Lena Grove?"

He stood quietly and listened. She was not looking for an answer. Rose was in a mental fog.

"Faulkner said, 'She was the captain of her soul.'"

"You can be as well, Rose."

"I have been," she smiled. "All my life."

"Then, it's time to come down from there."

"Don't you see, Detective," Rose continued. "If I listen to you and come down now, after all of this, you will be the captain of my soul."

"And you would never have that, would you?"

"This is my last sunset, Frank Braun," she announced. "I hope you don't mind me calling you Frank."

"Rose, rethink what you are about to do," he said. "We have much more to do together. More things we need to talk about to finish what we have started. You are very important. You are needed. Jacob needs you more than ever. You know he will be lost without you."

"You're the first person to ever tell me that, sir."

"It is true," he assured. "You must know that. Jacob needs you now more than ever."

"There are three graves just feet from where you stand…next to the silo," she described. "Look closely at those three fence posts on the east side of the pen. You will see small crosses carved into the posts…near the bottom. Straight out from those three posts you will dig. You'll find Wyatt, Iris, and the baby girl. Wyatt and Iris will be wrapped in brown nylon tarps, secured with duct tape. Next to them you will find the baby.

Inside the house, you will find mother and father. They were cremated. Their urns are in their old bedroom, on the tall dresser. I placed a small leather bag just inside the door leading into the silo. Inside that bag you will find my personal journal. It corroborates everything I have told you. There is also a crude hand-drawn map of the grave site. That will help you find them. There is other evidence inside the pouch that will help you find the entire truth. Perhaps, things you would have never considered."

"I'll make sure I get it."

"And while you're inside the silo, you will see several large wooden planks laid across the bottom," she explained. "Lift those up and look down inside the hole."

"The motorcycle?"

"The motorcycle."

"Come down now, Rose, and we will go to my office," he said. "My team will take care of everything here, everything you just told me about. Let's go get Jacob and we can leave together. You still have Jacob."

"The sunlight has faded," Rose whispered. "It is time for you to clean up this mess."

"We'll get it done," he promised. "I can still help you, Rose."

"Could you imagine a woman like me in prison?" Rose scoffed.

The irony of life's long march, colliding with imminent death, pierced the fresh country air. Braun sensed the inevitability. Time had finally ceased within the fading glow of the setting sun.

FIFTEEN

ROSE PORTRAYED A SENSE of relief, smiled, and watched how the sun began to disappear below the horizon, bringing a shadow over the unplanted dirt. Braun had not noticed, but at the top of the old tin roof of the silo, well behind her, Rose had tied an old hemp rope to a steel eyelet welded at the apex of the roof. Twelve feet long, two inches thick, a rudimentary, but effective, noose was fashioned at the other end of the rope. The end Rose now held in her hand and slowly placed around her pulsating neck. Braun looked back toward the car and noticed Jacob walking toward the silo.

"Stop right there, Jacob!" he shouted. "Don't come any further."

Jacob hesitated. As Braun turned again and lifted his eyes upward, Rose took one step forward into the welcoming void. No more words. No more explanations. When the long-slackened rope reached its end, the weight of her body cinched the noose as tightly as her neck muscles would allow. Braun heard the snap. He thought of Wyatt. Of Iris. He turned his head slowly toward the west just as the sun dipped entirely below the horizon line. As he watched the bright glow of orange fire vanish, Rose's lifeless body twitched without restraint, until her central nervous system surrendered. The silo held her physical form high in the air like a tree holds onto a fractured branch.

Detective Braun notified central dispatch to send the crime scene investigation unit. The team would be on their way. He would direct them to the pen, and silo, from which Rose dangled in the pending darkness. The coroner would do what coroners do. The proverbial wheels were set into motion. As Rose herself would have ironically appreciated, the mess would soon be cleaned up. Jacob ran far enough to the edge of the silo and looked up. Aunt Rose gently swayed, as if a lifeless human replica hung in effigy. There was that stillness again. That kind of stillness confirming the worst. He had seen it before. This time the stillness belonged to the woman that saved him and raised him. Right or wrong, she was the one that chose life for Jacob as he came into this world screaming, struggling, and surviving. Two and a half pounds of unadulterated innocent dependency. Vulnerable. Defenseless. Powerless. Why did Rose hold all the control when it came to life and death? Even in her own demise. Why did it seem so easy for her to adjudicate that ultimate decision?

DETECTIVE BRAUN and Jacob backed down the weed-riddled limestone driveway. Braun turned and headed down Old Johnson Road, for the last time, away from the farm. Jacob looked out ahead. A string of headlights approached the farm. Men and women arriving to go to work. Digging. Searching. Wondering. Wondering, what secrets the black earth held. What would they find? The farm seemed unfamiliar to Jacob now. It reeked of death. After all these years this was the first time his brain allowed him to smell it. There was a deep darkness that hovered over the silo. The place that held him prisoner, yet allowed him to take refuge so many times. Soon, there would only be artificial lights. Spotlights. Bright lights. Lights slicing through the blackness, giving a synthetic pathway to illuminate their morose work. Those muddy graves to be disturbed after years of slumber. Jacob looked back, then forward again, to the road in front of him, then over at Frank Braun as he quietly drove.

Braun's phone rang. He answered. It was the head of the search operation.

"Frank. We've dug up the graves," he said.

"What did you find?"

"Two adult remains."

"Wrapped in tarps?"

"Yes. Wrapped in tarps."

"What else did you find?"

"One small grave. Separate, but nearby."

"And…"

"Odd burial."

"How so?"

"There are two plastic bags," he described. "It was what we found inside the bags that you'll find interesting."

"What's that?"

"We cleaned the dirt off the bags so we could see inside, but that didn't work," he explained. "So, we had to cut them open just enough to see the contents."

"What did you see?"

"A box," he described. "A boot box."

"Any markings?"

"Red Wing," he said. "It's an old Red Wing work boot box."

"Large enough for a baby's body?"

"A very small baby, yes."

"It's inside," Braun predicted. "Be careful. Handle the box with care. Handle everything you find with care."

"I'll treat them with the same respect I would treat my own family, Frank."

"Thanks," Braun said. "I knew you would."

Braun hung up the phone. He looked over at Jacob. He was looking out the window. Counting the telephone poles. Jacob never spoke. Braun knew he overheard what was said. Avoiding the pain. Avoiding the truth. Avoiding the past. Avoiding Frank's eyes. Jacob knew he was the last of the Weavers.

"Were they found?"

"We found them all," Braun answered.

The two men continued driving down Old Johnson Road. Looking straight ahead. The darkness had fully replaced the light of day. Silence seemed appropriate. They both allowed it. Braun, now that he was older, had learned that silence was better at times like this. The quiet was interrupted by Braun's phone ringing. It was Catherine Thomas. She got wind of the crime scene at the Weaver's farm. Braun hadn't had an extra second to call her.

"Detective Braun," he answered.

"I heard what's going on at the Weaver's place," she said. "Nice work."

"You know about the three bodies?"

"Three, huh?" she sighed. "This solves a lot of cold cases, Braun. How is your guy holding up?"

"He's handling it. For now," Braun answered, "but, he knows his future is hanging in the balance. I told him it was all up to you now, Catherine."

"No pressure," she laughed. "I called to tell you to release him."

"Release him?"

"Yes. I am planning on dropping the drug possession charge."

"So, the three strikes law won't stand?"

"No three strikes," she said.

"When everything settles, he'll realize how important that is," Braun stated. "Right now, he's in a little shock."

"Take whatever time you need to wrap things up," she said. "Then, you can finally get on with retiring, Frank. I cancelled the morning arraignment, by the way. I will talk to you soon."

Braun closed his phone and turned towards Jacob. "You're a free man."

"Free? The dope charge is dropped?" Jacob asked, looking at Braun. He turned his gaze back out of the window.

"Where will you go from here?" Braun asked as they approached the police station. "Do you think you will ever go back to the farm?"

"Not for a while," he said. "But, sooner or later I'll need to go there."

"Do you think you'll sell?"

"Right now, my mind tells me to," he replied, "but, my heart says that was the only place I ever called home. Maybe I could do something good with that old farm. I just won't know for a long time."

"Maybe you can rent a place here in town for the time being," Braun suggested. "Get the farm issues straightened out. I'll know more about our investigation within a week or so. That may help you make some decisions, Jacob."

"You may not know this yet, Detective," he said, "but, do you think you will be charging me with Wyatt's death?"

"I don't see Ms. Thomas considering that," he replied. "I can't imagine that ever happening."

"But you don't want me to go too far, do you?" Jacob assumed.

"I think, for now, sticking around town would be a good idea," he said. "I would like us to stay in touch. We'll get coffee. There may be some things I can do to help you out."

"I'd like that."

SIXTEEN

DETECTIVE BRAUN PARKED his car in front of the police station. Jacob got out and began to walk down the sidewalk, away from the car. He stopped and turned toward Braun. It seemed like Jacob wanted to say something, but wasn't sure what. He was lost in thought. Like that runaway kid years earlier. Jacob had nowhere to go. He was on his own now and had to find his way. Jacob remembered Braun suggesting the local motel down the street, temporarily.

Braun went straight to his office, and sat down at his desk. He turned on a lamp. It was the only light on in the office. For once in thirty years, he realized his desk was clean. He did not recall what it looked like before. Two boxes on the floor were filled with his personal belongings, ready to go with him into retirement. He couldn't help but think of baby girl Weaver as he looked at the boxes. *What would have become of her?* Braun noticed the scarred and faded leather bag left to him by Rose. Inside, he found a thick journal, entries from as far back as the late 1950s. It would take days for him to sift through every page, but it would be worth his while. What would he find? Rose's life in her own words? Rose's sorrows. Her thoughts. Her confessions?

Tucked beneath the journal, was a small plastic bag. Inside the bag, protected from the corrosiveness of time, was a single newspaper article. He carefully unfolded the brittle edges. The paper was thin and flimsy, yellowed by age. Crispy and ragged at the corners. He immediately searched for the date: 12 May 1958. The article described the unfortunate, but accidental, death of a two-year old boy named Mark, which occurred on the Weaver farm, just off Old Johnson Road.

The article explained how Mr. and Mrs. Weaver had left the farm for a brief period, during the day, leaving little Mark in the care of his older sister, Rosemary. She made the fatal decision to bathe her two-year old brother. Innocent and regrettable were the two words chosen by the author of the article. The toddler drowned when his sister, Rosemary, appeared to have left the bathroom and became distracted, leaving the child all alone. He was the only son of John and Esther Weaver. There was speculation by the coroner that Rosemary became sidetracked from her child care duties, when she began to play with her younger sister, Iris. It was then the accident occurred. The investigation was brief and the findings unremarkable. The death of a child was heartbreaking to a small community. No one was shocked when the drowning was ruled accidental. The sad article ended with words of empathy towards Rosemary, a young girl that would have to live with such a preventable tragedy.

An article such as this may have disappeared into the history of the Weaver family farm, along with all the other recent revelations. Braun noticed that Rose chose to leave an incontrovertible clue for him, just before he walked out of the door for good. He realized that there was one crime in her life that she could not bring herself to openly confess.

Amongst the written text, within this single fading artifact, Rose acknowledged her worst crime. She had taken a black marker and circled the word *accidental*. He read further. Rose had taken that same marker and drew a straight line directly through the final five words of the article: *Rose was not to blame*.

FRANK REALIZED his mind and body were completely sapped of the ability to take in what had occurred over the last several hours. He needed to find a quiet place to unwind. A hot cup of black coffee. His perspective on the world had changed in many ways. New beginnings waited. Painful memories from a distant time had not been resolved. Memories he thought he had buried, within the deep jagged crevasses of the unforgiving landscape of life. Where does he go from here? How does he reconcile the path that brought him to this place in time?

He pulled up to Maggie's Café. There was only one other vehicle in the parking lot. It was an old Chevy truck. It sat alone at the end of the lot, the very last spot, facing the café's largest picture window. He walked in and saw Maggie behind the counter. She smiled. At the farthest booth, tucked in the corner next to that big window, sat the old man. On the table next to him was a torn and tattered, beaver felt Stetson cowboy hat. An eagle feather protruded from the fraying hatband. It was hard to distinguish the color. Between a gray and dirty white. It had seen better days. The old man had too. He tilted his head upwards, slightly to the left, glanced over toward Braun and acknowledged his presence with a slight nod. He then turned back again to continue peering through that picture window. Something about the old man drew Frank toward him. Perhaps, it was Frank's impending retirement. There was something about the old man's demeanor that spoke to Frank's brittle state of mind. There was no reason to ignore him. They were the only two patrons in the place.

Frank walked over to the booth and stood for a moment. The old man looked up.

"Would you mind if I joined you?"

"It's a free country," the old man grinned, with a smile that no longer possessed all the teeth God had intended.

Maggie brought Frank a hot cup of coffee and a slice of homemade blueberry pie. She knew what he had come in for. Frank looked down at the old man's plate. He noticed the yellow egg stains, crumbs from some toast and a greasy spot left by a salty sausage patty. *Breakfast for dinner*, he thought. Maggie poured a refill for the old man. He drank it black, too.

"Some big goings-on up at the Weaver farm, ay?" The old man contemplated.

"I'm Frank Braun, by the way." He reached his hand toward the old man.

"I know who you are."

"I'm not sure how to take that."

"Take it any way you'd like." The old man looked out the window. "Didn't mean nothing by it."

"How was your food?" Frank asked, trying to misdirect the questions about the Weaver farm.

"Maggie's food is always good," the old man said, pushing his plate to the edge of the table. "But I reckon you already knew that."

"Just making small talk."

"That mess you got up at the Weaver's place will make a man want to talk about nothing," he said. The old man gently pushed his hat off to the side. "Hot black coffee and a smile from Maggie won't make the Weaver case leave your mind anytime soon."

"You seem to know a lot about the Weavers," Frank stated.

"I know something about that place," he said. "Do I know the truth? Who knows for sure? The truth these days is downright elusive."

Frank didn't want to talk. He wanted to listen. The old man had things to say. Things he knew. Frank didn't want to hear his own voice. *Give it a rest*, he thought. *Let the old man speak.*

"Your truth, my truth, their truth," the old man lectured. "There ain't no such thing as the actual truth anymore. Two plus two can equal five nowadays. If ya shout it loud enough. Don't disagree or you'll hurt somebody's feelings. Ya don't want that. Ya might get sued. The world is upside down, if you ask me."

"I get what you're saying."

"I've been around a long time," the old man noted. With some pride, but a dose of regret, too. "How old are you? You're still a young man."

"I'll be turning fifty-seven soon," Frank answered, realizing he sounded just like Jacob, when they first met. "How old are you, if you don't mind me asking?"

The old man turned his head, looking for Maggie. He found her, squinting through his hazy cataracts, coming out of the kitchen toward the counter.

"Maggie!"

"Yes, Nick," she replied.

"Is it 2006 yet?" he wondered.

"It's 2005 still."

"Alright, then. I was born in 1920."

"You are eighty-five Nick. I could have told you that if you'd just asked."

"I like to figure it out in my head now and again," he grinned with those teeth. "It keeps my math skills up."

Frank looked out the window at the old man's truck sitting there. It seemed as though it patiently waited for his return. Like a trusty old dog.

"How do you know about the Weavers?"

"I've known about the Weaver family farm for many years," he said. "I spent almost ten years, from fifty-six to sixty-five as the Sheriff of this county. Got elected. I wasn't much of a cop. Just a farmer that decided the county needed a sheriff that would listen."

"So, you had some dealings with the Weavers?"

"I know some things you don't know."

"Such as?" Frank pried.

"I know the real story about those girls."

"The girls?"

"Iris and Rose."

"What'd you know about them?"

"They was adopted into that family."

"I never knew," Braun responded.

"It was a tragedy," the old man remembered. "Not many people knew, but I knew. Cause I was the Sheriff."

"I don't know the story."

"The Weavers adopted those girls. Through their church. They come up from Missoura," he explained. "The girl's parents died in a murder suicide."

"Their father killed their mother?" Frank assumed. He knew he shouldn't.

"No, no," the old man corrected. "The other way around. Mama killed their papa. She stabbed him in the chest, right there in bed, as he slept."

"You don't see that very often."

"Found mama out in the barn. She'd hung herself from a rafter."

"Did Iris and Rose see it?"

"The mother had dropped those girls off at the church earlier in the day," he went on. "She planned it, so the girls would be taken care of. Who knows what the girls learned about it when they got older."

"The Weavers thought they couldn't have their own children, I suppose?" Frank wondered. "So, they adopted those orphan girls through the church?"

"That's the story." The old man took a sip of his coffee. "God eventually gave them Mark. He was their only biological child. That was the case I handled. When Mark drowned in the bathtub, the girls were the only two at home. They trusted Rose."

"You investigated it? Decided it was an accident?"

"I didn't decide anything. I couldn't prove otherwise. Who was there watching the boy bathe? Was it Rose? Was it Iris? Were they both there? Did they both leave him alone in that tub? How in God's name do you determine that from talking to youngins like that? I wasn't trained how to interview kids. It was a different time back then. Things were done different. The community thought it was an accident. The paper ran with it. What would I have done to a couple little girls like that? I had to leave best alone. I had my own opinion. All I can tell you was Rose didn't seem that upset about the whole thing."

The old man unexpectedly quit speaking. Went completely silent. He began to gaze out of the window. Lost in the past. In regret. His truck still sat in its space. Like it was simply waiting for his return.

"There's nothing you could have done," Frank consoled the old man. "If it makes any difference now, after all these years, you were right about Rose."

The old man never heard a word. He just stared. Frank stood to go. The old man didn't seem to notice him leave the booth. Frank walked up to the counter and Maggie met him at the cash register.

"What was the old man's bill, Maggie?"

"Eight dollars and fifty-two cents."

"Do me a favor and take him a piece of that blueberry pie. Add it to my bill. I'll take care of his, too," he said.

"Okay, but he's got plenty of money, Frank," she stated. "He doesn't need any charity. You know who that is, right?"

"Not quite sure."

"That is old man Johnson. Nick Johnson. He owns all that farmland to the south of Old Johnson Road. Thousand acres. The road was named after him."

"You don't say? I got his check anyway," he smiled, as he turned back to look at the old man one more time. Frank handed her a twenty. "Keep the change, Maggie."

ACKNOWLEDGEMENTS

A HUGE DEBT OF GRATITUDE goes to my cover/interior designer, Christian Storm, who's creativity was boundless. He became a valuable advisor regarding many issues, going above and beyond the cover and interior design. I would like to thank my editor, Ellen Coughtrey, who provided a detailed analysis of my book and suggested various ways to shape my story without affecting my writing style.

I want to thank Shannon Shumrak and Joanne Arford who read my book early on, offering insights, comments, and encouragement. Thank you to all of my family and friends that shared their valuable opinions regarding my cover design choices. They all helped me come to a final decision.

I appreciate my sons, Ryan, and Kurt, who are avid readers and always share their critical thoughts regarding books and authors. This impacts my style of writing. Their input is always refreshing.

Finally, I want to thank my wife, Diane, for taking this writing journey with me. She stood by my side through all of the twists and turns this novel had to offer.

ABOUT THE AUTHOR

G.S. HEIST spent thirty-one years in law enforcement. He retired a Captain, in charge of the Criminal Investigation Division, where he developed expertise in several areas of investigation. He graduated from the FBI National Academy. He began writing fiction after retiring, using his imagination derived from years of investigating real crimes. He and his wife now live outside Chicago.

Made in the USA
Monee, IL
17 August 2024